BAR BALTO

Joël, AKA 'the Rink' because he's so bald you could skate on it, is the very unpopular owner of the only bar in town — so unpopular that when he is found dead, it's not so much a question of who did kill him as who didn't. His customers certainly had plenty of motives . . . In a series of monologues, the locals tell us their stories in their own, very different voices. As the tension mounts and we're still none the wiser, the ending — in the form of Joël's final confession — is as shocking and tragic as it is unexpected.

SPECIAL MESSAGE TO READERS

THE ULVERSCROFT FOUNDATION
(registered UK charity number 264873)
was established in 1972 to provide funds for
research, diagnosis and treatment of eye diseases.
Examples of major projects funded by
the Ulverscroft Foundation are:-

- Children's Eye Unit at Moorfields Eye
  ;pital, London
  e Ulverscroft Children's Eye Unit at Great
  nond Street Hospital for Sick Children
  iding research into eye diseases and
  itment at the Department of Ophthalmology,
  .iversity of Leicester
  ιe Ulverscroft Vision Research Group,
  ïtute of Child Health
  n operating theatres at the Western
  ιthalmic Hospital, London
  Chair of Ophthalmology at the Royal
  ralian College of Ophthalmologists

help further the work of the Foundation
ιaking a donation or leaving a legacy.
:ontribution is gratefully received. If you
like to help support the Foundation or
re further information, please contact:

ULVERSCROFT FOUNDATION
Green, Bradgate Road, Anstey
Leicester LE7 7FU, England
Tel: (0116) 236 4325

website: www.foundation.ulverscroft.com

FAÏZA GUÈNE

BAR BALTO

Complete and Unabridged

ULVERSCROFT
Leicester

First published in Great Britain in 2012 by
Vintage
London

First Large Print Edition
published 2013
by arrangement with
Vintage
The Random House Group Limited
London

A catalogue record for this book is available
from the British Library.

ISBN 978–1–4448–1679–2

Joël, aka Jojo, aka the Rink

It's Joël Morvier to you, and I've decided to tell this story in my own words. Thirty years I've been surrounded by newspapers, so there's no pulling the wool over my eyes. I can see how they twist the facts. Rather trust my own mouth.

I'd have turned sixty-two in April, twelfth of the month. I'm telling you that as a point of fact. I've never celebrated a birthday in my life.

They say I'm not an easy man to like. I'd say I didn't get as much love and sympathy as I deserved. As for the slurs, I'm no racist. I've just got values, and clearly that bothers some people.

I'm exactly as nature's factory turned me out. I've heard it said I'm the unfeeling sort, but there weren't many choices to start with. Still, nothing ever kept this car off the road. Made in France, I might add.

The way they go on, you'd think we had to get upset about every kid out there who's ever been raped.

I see the images on TV like everyone else: the bombings, the accidents, the hurricanes

1

and those old fogeys dying from the heat. Nothing doing. They don't affect me.

I lost my dad when I was quite young. But it's not like I'm the only one. Dads, they've all got to die some day. I'm not saying this for the sympathy trip, I'm just explaining.

So I lived with my Uncle Louis in the place over the bar for a few years. Then he went and snuffed it too. Cancer. My old man's death was as stupid as his life. Hunting accident. Mind you, everything was an accident with him, including me.

Our family's lived in Making-Ends-Meet for over fifty years now. It's got a population of about four and a half thousand, and it's stuck on the end of an RER line. Somewhere you'll never set foot.

Everybody round here knows me: Jojo, or 'the Rink' for the regulars. That's my nickname, supposedly because my bald patch is shiny enough to skate on. Still, it only happened recently — you should've seen my mop as a teenager. From behind, I looked like Dalida. I keep my hair long for the memories, even though there's this wasteland on top. I was the owner of Bar Balto. And yes, I know, you'll find Baltos all over France; let's just say we didn't rack our brains for the name. It's the local bar-tobacconist-newsagent's. The village lung. And vomit bag.

For years I've played the on-hand shrink. Spent whole evenings listening to them whingeing on about their shitty problems and dishing out their dirty jokes. My bar would make a mental-health ward look like a tea room. I used to try raising the level of conversation, but it never got any higher than the dole.

Each time I turned to my left I'd see Claudine, leaning on the bar, always in the same place. She spends so much time in that spot you don't notice her after a while. Everyone round here calls her the Black Widow. Word is she poisoned her husband a few weeks after they got married. Laced his pumpkin soup with insecticide. Whenever she's had one too many, she's got a thing for taking her clothes off — starting with her tights. I'll spare you the details.

Someone who felt sick at the sight was Yves Soninlaw, the son-in-law of the Mayor of Making. I'm not pulling your leg, that's his name, Soninlaw. He confided in me once that he'd never backed his father-in-law; just couldn't take standing in his shadow. I was the only person who knew that Soninlaw voted Commie.

One day, early last summer, he got me to order in a bodybuilding magazine, on subscription. You know the sort, for fitness freaks, whole pages of protein ads, the kind you'd use for beefing up prize cattle. Photos of tanned lads with big muscles and oil all over them. Soninlaw was hooked in no time. Couldn't get enough of them. I didn't want to know the rest. Just thought, there goes another poof.

My highlight of the day used to be around seven o'clock, when Madame Yéva dropped in to buy her Gauloises Blondes. Blow me, she's well stacked. No two ways about it, she's a good-looking woman. Always leaving this waft of perfume behind her, like a big pink cloud, a cloud of love. The sweetest scent that makes time stand still at the bar. Now, I don't want to get soppy here, but Madame Yéva is something else. The kind of woman who makes you feel inspired. Once or twice, I even put my hand on her bum — nice and subtle, mind. She took it badly. I made out I didn't do it on purpose, but she kicked up one hell of a fuss. Screaming in my face, calling me every name under the sun, and all the time I was just thinking how sexy she looked when she got feisty. She lives with three men and they're all as bad each other. Two sons: trouble in a baseball cap, and a mongol. Plus a husband in a shell suit who's addicted to the lottery. I reckon she must stay with him because of what he can do in the sack. Even so, it takes some imagining.

My Yéva's the only thing I'll miss.

I'm lying in a pool of my own blood here, starkers; you wouldn't believe the position I'm in. I was expecting to see my whole life flashing before me, like a film, but that's bollocks. All I can hear are voices.

Tanièl, aka Tani, Turkey Boy or Lazy Bugger

I'm not Turkish.

They don't get the difference. They're always calling me 'Turkey Boy'. But I'm not Turkish. I'm Armenian. Well, on my mum's side.

My name's Tanièl. My old lady calls me 'lazy bugger' and 'shithead' most of the time. For school it's Daniel, and for my mates it's just 'Turkey Boy'. If my grandad could hear them, he'd come back from the grave and smash their faces in. Personally, I ain't got no problem with Turks, they've done nothing to me. But we're not so keen on them in my family, except no one's ever explained why. My old lady, right, when she doesn't want to do something, she says: 'I'd rather sleep with a Turk.' So then you know she's not going to do it, for real, because the way she sees it that'd be worse than dying. Her brain's rinsed, man.

It's jarrin', all this 'Turkey Boy' stuff. When we go for a kebab at the station, my boys pack me off to talk in Turkish if the chef messes up our order, but shit, I don't even speak that language. Then again, I don't speak Armenian either.

They're jealous because I've banged Magalie, the blonde girl from Acacia Street. They were all sniffing her out. Especially Ali. He's new around here but he's Muslim and from Marseille, so he gets respect. He can't get enough of taking the piss out of people. I ain't no fool, I know he does it to take the attention off him. In the looks department, you see, Ali's butterz. The girls are always teasing him about his big nose. They say it's taken over his face, staged a military coup. That's how come he's got his nickname: 'Dictator'.

Still, he's got everyone in the palm of his hand. The gift of the gab, that's what it is. I'd like to be good with the chat too, but it's hard for me. Ali reads books, straight up. How weird is that? I reckon wifeys get turned on by a guy who reads. They're thinking he'll be open-minded and everything. And I don't mean a bloke like the Rink, who makes out he's some intellectual just because he reads *The Parisian* every morning.

My Marge hates Ali. I think she hates him the most out of all my bredrins. She's got this block about him, says he's got the face of someone who'd dig up the dead to pick their pockets. She calls him 'small balls'. When he whistles for me outside the window, she spits on him, and that makes Ali wild out. One day she only went and gobbed on his head: a big fat salty wodge of spit. It was like, WHAT? He couldn't believe it. The story did the rounds of the estate. And I felt 'nuff shame because of my old lady. She does my head in. I mean, she looks so easy-access does my Marge, you get me . . . She dyes her hair crow black and slaps on bright red lipstick. You can't get redder. And then she draws this fake beauty spot next to her mouth. Silly cow reckons she's Cindy Crawford. I know what they're all thinking when they see her. That she looks like the bucket pussies behind the station. And believe me, you can't say nothing: make one tiny remark and it's war. She gives us all this feminist bullshit about doing whatever she likes because she's a free woman. To be honest, I agree with her, but some free women dress normal, innit? The way I see it, all she's free to do is slap paint on her face and wear skirts that ride up her arse. I wish she looked more like Ali's mum. Now that's what I call a real mum. A bit fat. Wears long dresses. No make-up. Who just smells of soap and arks you what you want to eat. The kind who gets worried if you come home late. And looks after you when you're sick. A Marge you can respect, you get me.

I'll always remember that time when Ali got flu. I'd gone round to visit and his mum was putting orange-flower water on his face, on his chest and his neck, to bring his temperature down. Mine would never do that; her style's more fag-in-mouth, perfume that makes your eyes sting, and giving you the finger if you piss her off. Man, does she LIKE doing that. Sticking her finger in the air. I don't need to draw it, you've got which finger I'm talking about. She sticks it up, tall and straight, and says: 'Up yours! Go sit on this!' I'm telling you, she's out of order.

I'm a good son, apart from the messy bedroom and all the noise, but that's everyone, innit? She could at least listen to me when I'm talking to her. The skirts she wears are bare short. Shit, she's an old woman, and you can see her white thighs, you can see them a long way off. She didn't dress like that in the photos from Armenia. Her dad must've had her well under his thumb.

She's got no taste. I don't like her clothes, or the wallpaper in the lounge, or the curtains. I'm too embarrassed to invite Magalie over because I don't want her to see our Marge, or the tablecloth in the lounge, or the couch with its tassels, or my old man slumped on it.

I grew up with my boys on the estate. I'd head over from these endz to chill with them at night, even if I wasn't meant to. We caught some serious jokes there. Course, my mum wanted me to hang out with my neighbours instead, the neeks with the nice houses. We're talking the kind of person who hides their test paper with their elbow, to stop you copying them.

To start with, the guys from the estate were thinking I'd got dough because I live in a house. Being here seemed cool to them. They'd go: 'At least you've got the station close by and the town centre.' Yeah, right. Call this a town centre? There's the market in the square, the town hall, the post office, the pharmacy, the bakery, the police station and Bar Balto. That's it. If you wanna check you really are in 2008, you've got to hop on a train and get far away from here.

Talking of which, it's thanks to the RER that I got to make my move on Magalie. I'd seen her around for a few weeks, thought she looked fit. Then, one evening, I followed her back from the station, and when we made it to her street I said how about it, you and me? I took her for a drink at the Balto, but that bastard Joël decided to show her up. He was going on about how Magalie's dad wouldn't be happy. She told him she didn't care and

10

he'd be better off looking in the mirror, she didn't like ugly guys. That arsehole started yelling how people weren't wrong when they called her a filthy slut. Her eyes were all welling up so we decided to jet. I could've merked him that day, but it was my first time with Magalie and I didn't want her thinking I was an animal or something. After all, Joël's the kind of moron you only come across once or twice in your life. Magalie was so mad at him, she went and pissed in front of the bar window just before opening time every day for a week after that. Yeah, all right, so she's got a screw loose, but haven't we all?

Anyhow, you know that reputation blondes have? Well, it's not wrong. It wasn't like she was tough to crack. Bit of sweet talk in her ear, sorted. At the end of the day, linking with a wifey ain't difficult. What really does it for them, I've noticed, is being number one in your life. They want to feel they're the best; that they mean more than the rest. You've got to come up with stuff like: 'Out of all the girls I've known, you're the only one who gives me butterflies. I'm telling you, it never happened to me before, it's the first time I've felt like this . . . ' All that bull, they lap it up. You send 'nuff texts the first few days, so she's really in there, because girls think it's romantic. But at the end of the day it's just cheap, innit? Oh, and she can reread them at night while she's fantasising about you; so basically she's drooling over your face and you're just trying not to run out of phone credit. I've got it down to a smooth technique. The time always comes, yeah, when she complains you're not sending as many texts as before: that's when you've got to be right on it, tell her you prefer seeing her for real. Beginning of phase B: you start fixing up hot dates in out-of-the-way places. Like car parks at night. If you can get past this phase, you're king of the hill.

But with my girl it ain't just about that, we have good times together too. She's got pretty blonde hair, dainty fingers, skin that smells lemony and a gentle voice.

It's important that bit, I mean about having a gentle voice, because the way my old lady shrieks is JARRIN'. She blasts so loud it sticks to the walls, it really stresses me out. If she turns up at your place, she'll give you cancer of the eardrum.

My brother can't take it no more either. Yeznig, he's a bit mentally disabled. But you shouldn't trust appearances: our Marge is ten times more crazy than he is. My bro does stuff that's kind of unusual. Like he repeats everything he hears, word-perfect. He's got this incredible memory. He ain't much of a talker, but man can he spit those words back out again. I've never laid a hand on my little bro, I've never even hit him apart from maybe once or twice in the garden when we were kids. The last time I hit someone it was that beef at college. So, OK, I'll 'fess up, I've got a problem there, like I've got a temper on me. That's why I don't go to college no more. I beat up the Head of Year, Mr Leroy. He's been on sick leave for two months. To be honest, I'm sorry I did it now. He didn't even put in a complaint against me. My dad said: 'You jammy bugger, he must be a lefty!' Anyhow, I hope they can fix his teeth. I was meant to see an education adviser about finding me another college, but there ain't none round here. We're talking a half-hour train journey, so forget it. Even my little bro works. The other day, his Game Boy with his favourite game got jacked. I was *this* angry, man. I tracked down the guys and mashed them, one by one. I don't appreciate people taking the piss out of him.

He's no fool, my bro, he's just got habits. For example, he counts his teeth every time he's done eating; he's always worried about swallowing one without noticing. And another thing: he needs a special place for important stuff, that's why he's got a drawer full of batteries. It's for his Game Boy. Trouble is, he mixes up the new batteries with the flat ones.

Drives my old lady crazy: she has to get them all out to sift through. But with Yeznig, she never shouts at him. He's her baby.

I feel bad about it, but he spends so much time on his own, he ends up stuffing his face. He's getting fat and he plays pinball at the Balto for like bare hours. Because of being backward, he ain't got no sense of time. He muddles up before and after, past and future. My mum gets worried and sends me out to go and find him. That bastard Joël never keeps us in the picture. Sometimes it's the police who bring him back home. They know him so they're cool with him. I want to do something for Yeznig, but it's not like I can do much for myself. My parents don't even know I'm not going to college no more. I leave the house at seven thirty every morning with my Von Dutch bag, but there ain't no books or pens inside. Just my PSP, my tobacco, my skins and my spliff.

Magalie Fournier, aka the Blonde, the Slut or Turkey Boy's Wifey

Dunno what death looks like, but I'm telling you, I want it and I want it now. *Wanna die.*

My dad's confiscated my mobile, he says my bill's, like, *exploded.* He's exaggerating, as usual. I mean, come off it, 380 euros, it's not the end of the world.

So what am I meant to do now?

'You'll do without! We managed in our day!'

LOL. They make me laugh saying that kind of stuff. IMS if I wasn't born before Jesus Christ. Excuse me if I wasn't around for the Stone Age. I mean, PLZ, look, it's great for them if they used smoke signals to communicate when they were young, only maybe they're not up to speed with this but we're in 2008 here. My folks are stuck in a time warp. No kidding, they're still in the 1970s. Like HA-LLO! Anyone out there? Minitel with its Roman numerals on the keyboard is over! Wakey-wakey!

I've been shut in my bedroom since this afternoon.

If Tani calls, nightmare. We had a date for

six o'clock behind the car park at Conforama. He'll reckon I'm avoiding him.

What are they thinking? That being a parent gives them every right? It's not the UN here, you know. Plus, they've introduced this total ban on me cutting through the estate. Maybe they're scared I'll get gang-banged, or robbed or whatever else they've seen on TV. It's bad enough them setting a curfew — even though I'm sixteen — and forcing me to see a nutritionist once a week because I'm, like, open quotes, anorexic. I mean, why don't they just get me to spill my guts on Delarue's peak-time TV show while we're at it? Like I care. They're off their heads. *Whatever.*

It's been a nightmare ever since the old man found out I was dating a 'gypsy'. He doesn't think there's any difference between a gypsy, a Turk, an Arab and a monkey. He's a big racist, my dad. It's, like, totally embarrassing. Racism's *so* yesterday. Why can't he love people the way he loves his Labrador? Life'd be more of a laugh that way.

Oh, and that business of them finding the spliff in my rucksack didn't help matters.

So my mum's driving me crazy, going on every day about how I should be spending time with Karine Z, this girl from Simone de Beauvoir College. She's so stupid, she says

16

Karine's 'a nice girl to keep company with'. I mean, HA-LLO, what planet's she on? First of all, we're in 2008, like I've already said, and in 2008 you don't 'keep company with someone', you chill or jam or hang out together, but nobody keeps company any more. I'm telling you, they're stuck in the seventies, these people.

Anyway, whatever . . . So that bit of spliff they found in my bag? Well, it was Karine Z who gave it to me (that addict always has loads on her). And as for her being the right kind of 'company', yeah, nice one — she's so filthy she only went and got oral thrush at thirteen. I was still playing with my Barbie back then and Karine was already on boyfriend number five. If there was a sell-by date for human beings she'd already have gone off, like some mouldy old Brie at the back of the supermarket shelf.

Home's a war zone at the moment, shit happens practically every day. Next to this, Iraq's like Disneyland. So my mum's taken to popping tons of anti-anxiety *meds* and reading books that are supposed to give her advice on bringing me up. From *Understanding Your Teenager* to *How to Handle an Outburst That Gets Out of Hand* via *Coping Strategies for Living With Your Child's Anorexia*. Long live advice. She'd be better off reading *My Husband's Got High Cholesterol, He's Racist and We Don't Sleep in the Same Bed Any More*. LOL.

The guys who write these books, they think they can give us their crummy moral advice, but I bet their own lives aren't so great either. Or they'd be doing something else.

'I forbid you to see that pikey friend of yours, d'you hear me? I know what'll happen, I'll end up getting out my gun and firing it straight into his head, I'll knock his block off and yours too while I'm at it. What are you playing at? Huh? D'you want to end up like your sister? Is that it?'

Bam . . . whaddya know. He's talking about Virginie. My big sister who works in TV. She left this shithole town and our family for the big city. If you ask me, she did the right thing getting the hell out — as soon as I get a chance I'll do the same, for sure. My parents are so mad at her they could kill her. She ran off with a fifty-year-old producer, married, father of four, and to top it all he's a Moroccan Jew. The old man's brain couldn't handle it. Seriously, you should've seen his face. LOL.

To make him feel a bit better, Mum used to say to him: 'Tell you what, Jules, he could've been *black*.' The only thing the old man can do, when he's feeling angry or upset, is stroke Perno, our Labrador. It's that presenter on the one o'clock news who gave him the idea for the dog's name. My *pops* thought it was cute.

Whatever . . . I think my parents get all worked up about stuff because they're worried I'm going to clear off like Virginie, leaving them to their *meds* and the Labrador. But the worst that could happen, in their eyes, would be for me to get pregnant by a 'gypsy'.

Yéva, aka Madame Yéva, My Marge or My Old Lady

Hypochondriac, the doctor said at work. If that's the kind of diagnosis she comes up with, why did she even bother taking her science *baccalauréat*? She should try swapping that white coat of hers for my cooking apron, and we'll soon see if I'm making this up. Stupid cow, with her airs and graces: no prizes for guessing where I wanted to stick that stethoscope of hers. I bet she was jealous. I saw her when she asked me to take some deep breaths. She was eyeing up my chest. It's always the same reaction: women hate me, men can't get enough — what can you do? It's been like that since puberty.

On top of which the boss turns up at three o'clock, in the middle of my break, and finds I'm not at my desk. Of course I'm not. I'm in the toilets. Casting a bronze. Or dropping off the balance sheet, if he prefers, is that better for him? Because maybe he's a princess or something? Anyone'd think he never paid a visit to the bogs. I always allow myself ten minutes, and that's exactly when he decided to track me down.

I'm talking about our new department head, Joseph Frédéric. He'd come to give me a lecture about my so-called recurring record of sick days. I'm old enough to be that stuck-up number's mother, so it's hard swallowing a lecture from him. I mean, do I complain about him being ten minutes late in the mornings? Ten minutes, every day! I wouldn't dare work out how much that comes to, over time. I have to wait at the door for him every day, because he's got the keys. He refused to get a spare set made for me. Little prick likes to throw his weight around. But once you're over fifty, you put up and you shut up — and the wanker knows it.

Ever since he started with the company, he's banged on about revamping the admin department and modernising our working methods. So it's all about *process* and *scheduling and briefings*, if you please. The office is beginning to stink of America. Plus, he says I have to smile when I'm on the phone because, according to him, the person on the other end can hear the difference . . . Come again? I feel ridiculous smiling into thin air. All I can see in front of me is a wall and the kittens on the post office calendar.

He reckons he's the dog's bollocks just because he's got a gaggle of turkeys running after him. Grannies in their fifties dressed like old ladies, not even any make-up, licking his boots all day long. 'Can I get you a cup of coffee, Joseph?' . . . 'You're looking well today, Joseph, did you go away this weekend?' . . . 'Joseph, I've cleaned your computer screen!'

Makes me sick. Take Patricia and Simone, two of the biggest brown-noses I've ever seen. They're the kind of colleagues I'm up against. They tried being all chummy at the beginning, but I told them I wasn't interested in making friends. If I'm getting on that RER during rush hour, it's to do a job, not to cosy up to end-of-career Barbie dolls. As for the way they change the subject as soon as I show up in the office — 'My ears are burning,' I tell them. Cue their two-faced smiles. 'We weren't talking about you, we were talking about the President's new wife. Have you heard the latest?' Me: 'I don't give a monkey's about the President's new wife, OK? I'm too busy working myself to the bone to bring home the bacon!'

I clock out, I catch the train, I buy my pack of Gauloises at the Balto and I get home at the same time nearly every day, which just goes to show that nothing unexpected ever happens. As soon as I walk through the front door, life goes into black and white, it's such a drag. The old boy's got his arse wedged in exactly the same place in front of the telly. He's nearly made a hole in the couch. What am I saying? More like a ditch, with a backside like that.

I heard on the radio that for two hundred thousand euros you can experience zero gravity for three minutes, a hundred kilometres above the Earth. In other words, one day soon some bloke's going to blow the money I'll spend my whole life trying to scrape together in the time it takes to smoke a fag.

It wouldn't cost as much as that to make my dream come true, and I can tell you that for nothing. For once in my life, I'd like to find out what 'having a rest' feels like. Not the eternal rest. Though there are times I'd happily invite that one into my bed as well.

A bit of peace and quiet, is that too much to ask?

It's the RER from 5.17 a.m. to 12.35 a.m., every day. With all this noise, we might as well live next to an airport; at least then we could dream.

At work: Simone coming and going in the corridor, the sound of the coffee machine, the bogs right by my desk with their chorus of flushing water, the bleeping of the fax machine, the telephone ringing, Joseph's voice, the hum of the air con, the unhappy customers (and I know what I'm talking about, I'm responsible for registering the disputed cases). On top of which, the building site for the clinic behind our office revved into action last week, with Pneumatic Drills & Co.

At home: the telly's always on and, seeing as the old boy's hard of hearing, the volume's mostly turned up full blast. There's rap coming from the boys' room, all night long. It's mainly Tanièl, my older one, who listens to this music for gangsters. That shithead loves hanging out with trouble, the kind you see on telly, blacks and Arabs, preferably with shaved heads.

God, what have I done to deserve this? Just talking about it gives me palpitations. Who dumped this idiot husband on me? Buying a house thirty metres from the RER station! Practical and cheap, that's what he said. Oh, really? And all the time it's me who has to break my back paying off the mortgage.

If I'd listened to my father — may he rest in peace — I'd have married an Armenian with a bushy moustache, he'd have built me a house over there and I'd have left this dump a long time ago.

As for this one, glued to the telly like an insect on Rentokil flypaper: it's impossible to make him budge from there. Anyway, I've given up trying.

Back in April 1991, he was in the audience

for *The Price is Right,* this programme that was on at noon in those days. He loved it so much he still plays the video. You can see him for a split second up at the back, clapping like a big ninny.

Recently, he wanted to sign up for *Deal or No Deal* He dialled the number at 1 euro 54 cents a minute and got sent this complicated form he made me fill out. Measurements, profession, eye colour, hobbies . . .

It was a pain in the arse getting my tape measure round his flab. I filled in each box with my biro, but when we got to the one about his hobbies, the old boy dried up. It was like a computer bug. Nothing. Not a single idea in his head. We ended up putting 'scratchcards and telly'.

If it was just crappy programmes, things would still be OK . . . But no, Sir's got a gambling problem.

He has to play at least once a day. It's the only thing that gets him out of the house now. And once he's off, there's no counting on that pervert Morvier to rein him in.

Luckily, he's stopped going to the casino. Because in the old days he'd disappear off with his factory mates and bankrupt himself. He used to gamble like a lunatic all weekend, but it never hit home until the Monday.

Then his bank manager would call. 'Could

you please confirm that you've signed two cheques for four thousand francs each, sir?'

What a loser! It was like a bad comedy sketch round at ours. He would slap himself in the face and start blubbing: 'No way! I can't have done that! I swear to you, all I bet was fifty francs, tops!'

He even started suspecting his mates of nicking his cash, so he began to sneak off on his own, but I always found out in the end. The week after, another phone call from the bank and the same pantomime.

Worse than a kid. When he threw a wobbly, I wanted to stick my kitchen knife in his fat belly. He stopped just in time, I'm telling you. It gave me high blood pressure. Especially once when I caught him red-handed. Makes me feel ashamed just talking about it. It was a Saturday afternoon and he was playing battleships with his sons, who were just little kids at the time. 'Well, whaddya know,' I said to myself, 'lard-arse is looking after his sprogs! What's come over him?' Turns out they were playing for money! Can you imagine? I caught him laying bets against his own children. I was so mad at the bastard I wanted to jam those chips up his arsehole. What a disgraceful way for a father to behave. I got there in the nick of time, or he'd have made off with all their pocket money.

I read him the riot act in the end. He had to quit going to the casino. I allowed him one or two scratch-cards a day plus the football pools — I couldn't take those away from him, he wouldn't have survived. To make him surrender, I decided to double-lock my thighs for a while. Still, he held out for two months, which is astonishing for a lech like my hubby. He ended up going to the pigs to get himself banned from gambling. And it wasn't a moment too soon: I couldn't take it any more. I had to work twice as hard and do overtime with those silly bitches Patricia and Simone, not just for the mortgage but to help him pay back his overdraft. When the factory closed down, it was a real blow.

Since then, it's as if nothing matters apart from telly and the Balto. He spends a bit too much time in there on his stupid games, if you ask me. To be honest, I don't really like the place. The stink of beer and unemployment hits me the moment I open that door.

If it didn't mean slogging seven kilometres to buy my fags somewhere else, I'd never set foot in there. It hasn't escaped my notice that Morvier, the bar owner, likes eyeing me up in this really filthy way. One day, I nearly slapped him. He'd got right in there behind me, making out he was picking up some tickets off the floor, but it was just to grope my arse. Now, I know I've got curves in all the right places, and this gets some men in a right old state, but it's still no excuse. If he was attractive, he might just about get away with it. But Joël Morvier is one of the most repulsive men I know. Blokes like that are capable of the worst. He should be locked up or have his throat slit. I didn't tell Jacques about the incident, but if he found out he'd flay him alive. That is, if Sir could bring himself to get up off his fat bottom for his wife . . . Not that I need him. I'm not some pathetic housewife who relies on the man to sort it out. I can take care of my own business, thank you very much. In fact, seeing as I do everything by myself anyway, I should be claiming single-parent benefits.

If I could at least count on Tanièl. But he's no better, the little shithead. I have to spend half my time screeching at him. As for Yeznig, my baby . . . His disability's affecting him worse than before, what with puberty, the hormones and all that. His dad suggested he take himself down to the prostitutes, but he didn't want to go. What am I supposed to do? I'm dealing with two teenagers and an unemployed man, all hitting the skids at the same time.

Jacques, aka Jacko, the Old Man or Hubby

Third time he's been back on.

He's going for the jackpot of 10,300 euros today. No flies on him. Haven't seen such a strong contestant in three months.

Tight white polo shirt, trousers too short. Looks like he works in IT.

'Here's our champion: Didier, who's thirty-seven and from Wattrelos in the North. Didier works in IT. He's a big fan of cartoon strips and has collected over three thousand albums. He's also into Japanese poetry and travelling.'

So the host says to him: 'Where have you travelled?' And Didier goes: 'Scotland, because it's near to home but different at the same time. I go there as often as I can, with my wife Nathalie and our daughter Lea, who's thirteen and watching today.'

'Hello, Lea!' goes the host. And Didier pipes up: 'Fingers crossed for Daddy!'

Cackles like a turkey, wobbling his double chin right in front of the camera. Host's not laughing though. Must be the third programme he's recorded today. Looks dead on his feet.

Jingle.

'And now let's welcome the other contestants!'

Didier's on his guard. Reminds me of the neighbours' bulldog. Hands on the buzzer already. Lying in wait for his future enemies.

A small round ball with short legs bowls up. Looks like she's about to tip over. Tense smile, clutching her Virgin Mary pendant.

'Sylvette, who's forty-four and from Pessac in the Gironde, works as a secretary in a pensions department. She's already a granny twice over and is into stamp collecting and reading about Hungarian archdukes.'

'How's it going, Sylvette? Got a bit of stage fright?'

Reckon she's peed her pants. Presenter tries a joke to relax her. It doesn't work. She starts trembling.

'And now let's welcome Denis, who's twenty-three and from Marseille in the Bouches-du-Rhône. Denis is studying medieval history and he's into underwater diving and cetaceans.'

Two long thin arms, white body, floppy. He's wearing a shirt the wrong size, jeans the wrong size and a head — you got it — that's the wrong size too. Massive great skull, never seen anything like it. And God knows we had some physical deformities back at the factory. I'm talking case studies. Me and the lads used to wonder if they were born like that or if it was the job that did it. But this Denis, he's a Chernobyl-style champion.

Reminds me of the monsters in the science-fiction books I used to read as a kid. Didn't know Frankenstein was lying low in Marseille. Going diving with a head like that? It'd be like casting anchor.

The next contestant seems in a bit of a rush. Striped tie, small round gold glasses. Got to be ex-army, retired.

'And last up we have Yves, who's sixty-four and lives in the fourteenth arrondissement in Paris, a retired literature teacher who's also a former national cross-country skiing champion. These days, Yves is into Asian cookery.'

Nice bunch of people *into* their hobbies. Gets me down. More jingle.

TIN TAN TIN — TIN TAN TIN — TIN TIN TAN TIN TIN.

Bet Didier wins again and pockets the 10,300 euros. Last time, the finalist messed up on this question: 'Which planet in our solar system is more commonly known as the 'Evening Star'?'

The bloke just dried up. Stanislas, he was called, I remember because the presenter kept hammering it home. 'Dearie me! What happened, Stanislas? It was Venus!' Stanislas tried muttering something to save face, but it was all over. Must've mumbled: 'Of course. I knew that . . . '

Should've seen his mug when the final jingle was playing — he was this close to topping himself. Bet he didn't get a wink of sleep for weeks after.

Get themselves in a right old state, just for some *Larousse* dictionaries. Best-case scenario they leave with the big wine dictionary, worst case it's the dictionary of proper nouns. Or else they're a brainbox who comes back a hundred and thirty times, like Didier, to clear off with a nice bit of cash.

My life before was: job at the factory, caff behind the factory, friends from the factory, trips with the workers' union from the factory. So now, take out the word 'factory' and you can see what's left. Bugger all.

I hope my Tani carries on with his studies. Don't want him ending up like me, at fifty-six, on the couch.

Thick as a brick he is, so I'm not expecting him to end up as a doctor or anything, but a salesperson at Darty would be a start. They're well turned out over there, they smell nice and they sell flat-screen tellies. For the little one, though, there's no chance. He's scaled down, mentally. This year, he can get dressed by himself and he's stopped wetting his bed, so I guess it's not all bad.

Being out of work doesn't do me any favours, gets me thinking about the casino again. Just a little go on the slot machines would help me unwind, but I'm not allowed any more. I'm banned from gambling.

It's like making a formal complaint against yourself. You've screwed up once too many, you give yourself a blasting and then you ban yourself from ever doing it again.

I've only been back once. I flashed my ID and the bird went: 'I don't think so! You're banned from playing.' I gave her a hard time: 'Go-ooon, per-leeeze!'

I could see myself standing there, in front of her, pleading to be let in. When only the week before I'd been begging the pigs not to let me set foot inside a casino ever again. Crazy world. It's like an alcoholic 'banned from the bar' or a prostitute 'banned from the pavement'. All I've got left are my scratch-cards, my sports lotto cards and my Rapido at the Balto. Plus catching up with the ex-factory lads. We talk about the old days. But mainly about *that Monday*. We all got sent the recorded delivery letter laying us off on the same day. There were a few tears shed down at the post office, I can tell you. Even hulks the size of wardrobes, weighing in at a hundred kilos. Two hundred and fifty people out of a job just like that, two weeks before Christmas. Happy New Year, you poor sods!

Can't help dreaming about a big win, though; it'd solve all my problems. Every so often there's a glimmer of hope when I scratch a two-euro ticket and win two euros, because it means I can buy another one.

Jojo, the bar owner, couldn't care less about me. Got the face of a bastard. Seriously, it's written on his forehead, you can't trust him. 'Jacko!' he says to me, 'I've got a letter here from those nice people at the lottery. You've been putting so much cash their way they decided it was time to say thank you!' And then he sniggers behind his counter. As my darling wife would say, and she's never backwards about being vulgar: 'That guy's got the laugh of a dickhead.'

Told you! Didier's nabbed the jackpot. Jammy so-and-so bagged the loot in the final against Giant Head. Tight contest though. I'll see if he wins again tomorrow or if a new deformed specimen wipes the floor with him. Here we go, time for *Deal or No Deal*; it's the Poitou-Charentes region playing today. Thirty-something babe, nice body. Yéva'd shout at me if she could see me watching this. She'd say: 'Why're you watching that daft game?' I reckon she prefers the programme with the dictionaries; at least then she thinks I'm trying to improve myself.

Talking of which, she won't be long now. She'll shove the keys in the lock. The clock'll say 7.04 p.m. or, with a bit of luck, 7.15 p.m. if she's missed her train. She'll come in and her high heels'll go clickety-clack on the tiled floor. Then she'll call out: 'I'm back!'

Like I hadn't noticed with all that racket.

Then, same as every evening, she'll stick her mop of hair in the freezer and shriek: 'What d'you wanna eat?' She won't even give me a chance to answer before yelling: 'There's turkey escalopes!' So I'll have to eat turkey escalopes with no flavour. And if I'm stupid enough to start up on the subject of food, she'll throw a hissy fit.

'You don't like it? Well, why don't you go into the kitchen and fry a chunk of your fat arse? See what that tastes like! Just shut up and eat up. I should've listened to my father — may he rest in peace . . . '

At least the women on telly talk nice. My wife's vulgar. She makes me feel ashamed, I'm telling you, the way she mouths off like a lorry driver. Does my head in.

Marcel, our boss, often used to say: 'Silence is a woman's most beautiful jewel, but unfortunately she doesn't often wear it.'

Nadia and Ali Chacal, aka the Twins, the Marseille Posse or the Jackals

— Ali! I'm going first, for once!

— Go on then. What are you giving us? Your feminist bull: *We're-Not-Prostitutes-and-We-Don't-Take-It-Lying-Down?* Get on with it! Hurry up and talk!

— Look, the thing is, I'm tired of what people keep saying about our family, the rumours and all that. I want to tell the truth, for once. So, yeah, it's true our father works in the market. But he's not doing it on the black. He's got a licence like every other stallholder. He gets up early and he sells vegetables. Vegetables are good for your health. Even in the ads they say you should eat at least five a day.

— Get to the point.

— You said you'd let me speak, OK? Right, the next thing is we're not ten brothers and sisters, we're five. It's not the same. And I've had enough of people at college making remarks about family allowance benefits.

— Yeah. It's like a precipice.

— You mean a prejudice.

— Whatever you say, Miss Know-It-All. Go on then, sorry I spoke! I keep forgetting you didn't have to repeat the year at school.

— D'you mind not cutting me off every thirty seconds, Ali? I'm saying all this so people really understand who we are as a family. As far as I'm concerned, there's a lot of ignorance in this town. I mean, when Dad told us we were moving up to Paris, I was picturing the Eiffel Tower, the shops, the whole scene. I was expecting one big party and the only thing I'd miss would be the sea. But it's not Paris here, it's nothing. It's the countryside, and you've got to sit for an hour and a half on the train to get to the capital. We've got a proper house now, that's the only good thing. It's good because it means we're not on top of each other any more.

— It's mainly Mum who's happy about it. She's got a little garden so she's fixed up a vegetable patch. She grows mint and tomatoes.

— But if you're young, it's dead round here. You've fitted in, Ali, you've got your crew, but I don't like it. It's crap. There's just OAPs here — mainly old ladies — who must be really bored because all they do is gossip about everyone. If there's a tiny scrap of paper in the street it's automatically our fault.

If it wasn't for Mum, I'd have set the story straight long ago, old ladies or not. I'd have given them such a hard time about it — bam, they'd have had a heart attack.

— Listen to you! They're just going to think we're FOBs!

— You don't need me for that — they already think we're fresh off the boat, nothing new there. It's a shame Mum keeps quiet. She always does, Dad too, but not so much. Mum's always saying we've got to keep a low profile, behave like guests, not kick up a fuss, because it's not our country. Well, that's OK for her. But this *is* our country! We were born here! If she wants to stay a guest, that's up to her, but sorry, this is my home, even if it is the countryside.

— You shouldn't think everyone's against you, Nadia. They're not all racist. That's just paranoid, that is.

— Wow! Are we popping open the champagne, or what? So now you're trying out your fancy vocab on us? All that to impress the *roumis*. You're losing the plot, bro. Are you just blanking what goes down at the bar? Every time Dad goes to pick up his newspaper, the guy there, the bald one, he just chucks it at him, as good as throws it in his face. Like our money's dirty or something. And when he makes him a coffee, the

38

bastard deliberately fills it to the brim so it spills over. Dad's the one who told us about it. I'm not making it up.

— Dad needs to react, that's all. That's why people walk all over him.

— Look at you! If you were a real man you'd be the one to smash that *gadjo's* face in. We've got to defend our honour. We're not dirty people. Dad prays. He washes five times a day, including behind. So it's not for a guy like that who only has toilet paper, it's not for a stinking arsehole like him to walk all over Dad. How can he look down on Dad when he's the one with grimy black nails? They're the dirty ones, I'm telling you!

— It's just not my problem. Dad was born in the war, his father fought in the war, and so did his grandfather. He knows how to defend himself if he wants to. I'm all right here, I've made my friends.

— Yeah, let's hear it for your friends! If I remember right, it's your friend the Turk who jacked the girl you like? Hey? You got overtaken — that's like *big shame*!

— Shut up! No one asked you, OK? It's none of your business.

— Oh yes it is, course it is! And it gets on my nerves, big time. All that fuss for a little blonde bitch. She's in my class so I know what I'm talking about. The Magalie effect:

she only comes to school to show off her
different-coloured thongs and get the boys
drooling. She even turns on the charm for
our English teacher; I've never seen anything
like it. Who does she think she is? *Shame!* If
Mum knew, she'd disown you.'

— What's Mum got to do with this? Leave
her out of it.

— Yeah, well, let's just say that girl's got a
reputation. I wouldn't be seen dead with her.

— She's too pretty to be seen with you.
Just stay with your ugly girlfriends. No point
mixing things up.

— Get lost! You're no better. That's why
she wasn't interested in you, she preferred
your Turkish classmate with his spliff
aftershave. You're just jealous of him, end of.

— You're the jealous one. All you do is
criticise, but really you dream of having her
life. You're always dissing her: *the blonde this,
the blonde that* . . . Deep down, you want to
look like her. If you didn't have such a big
bum, you'd even borrow her thongs! You'd be
blonde, if you could be. It's like a hedgerow,
your frizzy hair, and even after a two-hour
straightening session you still look plain
weird.

— Up yours, I'm being myself. The same
person I was in Marseille. I don't need to
behave like the whites from the village. But

you drink alcohol like them and you want to go out with blondes. Oh, and while we're on the subject, what about your girlfriend Sabrina, if you can still remember her, that is . . . ? Or should I say ex-girlfriend? She keeps calling you at home, poor thing. I'm telling you, next time she rings I'll suggest she looks for another *gadjo*, it's better for her that way, I'll tell her the truth.'

— Mind your own life, Nadia. I'm a big boy now. I love Magalie, OK, and she'll see that. I'm no wasteman. When we moved here, we had a chance to start again from scratch, and I want to prove I can do it. I'll get what I want.

— Whatever you say, Mr Hero. When it comes to your life, I feel like I'm watching a Pakistani romantic movie, the kind Mum has on all the time. I'm just waiting for the big dance scenes now. You've got lots of space for running around and scattering your flower petals here, we're in the countryside, it's full of fields . . .

Yeznig, aka Baby, Fatty or the Spaz

This year, he started getting hair everywhere. Growing in every direction. In this place here, and there, most of all. Next week, I was thirteen. I was a big boy now. Even if Mummy says 'sweetheart', and she says 'my baby' too. On telly, they never show babies with hair, and in the street, in their prams, they wouldn't have hair either. I wasn't a baby any more. She doesn't want to stop with the baby. She'll say 'baby' to me and to Daddy she says 'bastard'. That's it.

One day, I'd like to make her fall downstairs or tidy her away in the fridge, where she'd hide my ice-cream cones. One day, maybe. She won't let me eat sweet things because the doctor says I was too fat but why is he so fat? If he's allowed to say I'm fat then he can't be fat. And he'll say to Mummy: 'Stop smoking, it's bad for you,' but one day I saw him doing it. A fat doctor who smokes isn't a proper doctor, or else he has to let everybody eat sweet things and smoke lots of cigarettes. If he says something like that again, I'm giving his eyes to the birds to eat. That's it.

I volunteer at HUW in the morning and I come home at night. HUW means: Helping Us Work. It's Arnaud, the director, who'll tell me that. He says he helps me but I'm the one who helps them: I'll stick labels on boxes all day long. The same thing again, again, again. Labels, boxes, labels, boxes. I'll be President of France, because he can be on telly and in the newspaper at the same time and he does what he wants, he gets on a plane, he goes to every country and he's got lots of money and sunglasses. But Joël, the pinball boss, he told me I'm never President in my life, he says: 'We've never had a mongol president in France,' and he laughs at me. Joël's more mongol than me. He's always touching his hair behind his head, he's scared it's falling out maybe. He's very hairy as well, under his shirt, in his ears, in his nose and on his fingers too. Another thing, he often scratches in his trousers. It's not clean. Mummy will shout in her voice when I will do it. 'No! My baby! Don't do that! It's disgusting!' So I didn't do it any more. I was doing it when she isn't there. Soon, when I was President, being hairy wasn't allowed.

Radio France, Paris Region

What happened last Friday night at the Balto, a sleepy bar in Making-Ends-Meet? That's the question the officers in charge of the investigation must answer after the body of Joël Morvier, owner of the premises, was discovered this morning: the police found him stabbed seven times in the stomach, with his face swollen up. Regulars and passers-by spontaneously rushed to the bar to pay their last respects to the man known affectionately by all as 'Jojo'. Tears, solemn faces and, above all, a sense of bewilderment. Everybody here is wondering who could have held a grudge against such a popular local figure. The investigation may only just be under way but the debate is already heated: with some pointing to a new serial killer, while others favour the idea of a night out gone wrong. With the first witnesses due to be heard at the police station this afternoon, Mayor Pierre Ledoux spoke into our microphone to reassure the people. 'Although no leads can be ruled out at this stage, there is no reason to believe that this is the work of a serial killer. Therefore, I would ask all residents to remain as calm as possible. This is a difficult time for Making-Ends-Meet, but we have experienced difficult times in the past and I have every confidence that my fellow citizens will get through this period, once again, as calmly as possible. Justice must be done and our contribution lies in being ready to face the truth, the whole truth.'

Joël, aka Jojo, aka the Rink

Gone eight o'clock this morning, the shutters were still down. My gaggle of alcoholics was getting impatient. They must've sensed something was up — I've always held that pastis drinkers had good instincts. It was the Black Widow who decided to call the police; after walking round the outside of the shop, she realised the day's deliveries had been left on the ground by the stockroom door.

They turned up straight away. Even I was surprised.

Vincent Bergues, aka Yellow Flash, was in charge of the troops. We call him Yellow Flash because he goes jogging on Sundays and, from the bar, you can see him speeding past in his tight-fitting Day-Glo yellow tracksuit. And he's not just any runner, either: this guy won the Oise road race back in 1994.

He's got the face of a man who takes things in hand. Square jaw, square shoulders, probably a square brain too, square as that van they turned up in. Brand new vehicle. I've always wondered why they splash out so much on their equipment. What with the drop in purchasing power and the social security deficit, now's no time to play at Don Juans in luxury vans. Especially since those layabouts don't have much to do round here. If it wasn't for me giving them a job's worth today, they'd be here in the bar anyway, buying their crosswords and sudoku magazines. It was magic when Bergues ordered them to open up the metal shutters, better than in a Western. This great cloud of light shining down on the bright red pool of blood all around me. Daddy Jean, if you could see me, you'd be a happy man: in all your years of hunting, I bet you never saw such a handsome prey.

Slowly, the light started to finger my corpse. I was a star, Elvis in the spotlight, for what was about to be the concert of the century. The crowd let out a roar so loud you could have heard it in Paris. The Black Widow fainted. I fancied a cigarette.

I want to describe this moment with as much poetry as possible. It's something that was sorely lacking in my life, so I'm trying to shove a bit into my death. An empty bar, the corpse of a modest man, a farandole of police hats and a few unemployed blokes chilled to the bone.

It all happened so fast, like in those adverts for life insurance where you see the seasons speeding by. For me, taking out life insurance was like getting married: more bollocks I avoided. You snuff it, you snuff it, end of story. And yes, I know what's going to happen next: the state will repossess my gaff; and it'll go to auction seeing as there's no heir. All the idiots round here'll miss me in the end, when some dodgy Chinese family takes over the Balto and starts serving up rancid spring rolls as the dish of the day and turning the cellar into an illegal sweatshop.

In no time, reinforcements showed up in yet more new vans, generously provided by the Ministry of Defence. They got on with what they call 'sealing off the area': cordoning it off with tensa barriers and pushing back the nosy parkers. What a stroke of luck for them, a story that'd make tomorrow's headlines. When it's on the TV news, I bet their wives'll video the whole thing for posterity.

About an hour later, the forensics team turned up. Blokes who knew what they were doing. Never seen anything like it. They put on protective gear to avoid contaminating the area and wore full bodysuits, gloves, over-shoes and masks. They were using metal tweezers in the room to collect a whole pile of muck that they stuffed into plastic bags. A bit later, there was even a photographer. Told you I was Elvis. It wasn't exactly *Paris Match* or *Voici*, but still. The police photographer papped me. I wanted to tell him I wasn't at my most photogenic, but it was the wrong time to crack a joke. I respect people who are doing their job.

The mob in front of my Balto was getting bigger. No fool, old Jojo. I chose the right day. It's Saturday. None of these cretins are at work, the few that do work, that is.

They'd all gathered in front of the window, hoping to satisfy their revolting curiosity. I was on the lookout for Yéva's face among the crowd of rats. Fancied giving her the eye one last time. Watching her light her Gauloise Blonde, then seeing that glorious smear of red lipstick she leaves on the filter every time. I've even collected her cigarette butts, kept them just as they were. I wanted her in my bed and if it weren't for me being dead, I might've persuaded her to follow me upstairs one of these days. I guess I botched it. But a cocktail didn't seem such a bad idea at the time. I'd mixed a special blend of rum and passion fruit. Something sweet, like her. 'Yéva on the Beach'. I didn't put it on the menu. It was supposed to stay between the two of us, but that bitch told me where to go when I suggested she try it. Not that she's even here now. Can't see she'd have anything better to do.

Her fat lump of a husband's made it. I can

see him all right, like a great elephant standing there; he's having a hard time keeping his balance with that big arse of his. He always looks like he's leaning backwards. He's holding a piece of yellow paper, tips for the horses. Worst thing is, he doesn't know the first thing about racing. It's pathetic. Since the Moulinex factory closed down, I've never seen him in anything but that green tracksuit with its European flag for the ten countries — dates back to 1986, it's written on the sleeve.

Last month, he scratched a winning Banco card at my bar, worth fifteen thousand euros. Bloody idiot buys five tickets a day, so he doesn't even bother checking any more. I kept an eye out while he was doing it. Bingo. All I had to do was wait for him to bugger off, and then scoop his winnings from the bin. How on earth did a loser like him land a bird like Yéva?

I didn't have as much luck as him. I never drew the right numbers. So I don't talk about it much.

There was Anne-Marie Freysse for thirteen years; blonde, on the large side. She was my girlfriend and my waitress, dual-purpose, as I used to joke with the boys. I liked her, I'll give you that; she kept her mouth shut and only opened it when necessary, meaning when I let her.

Another bonus: she didn't want children, can't think of anything worse myself. She and I got on well enough until the day she made off with an effing fair-ground type, a gypsy. A right shock to the system that was, but I was young, I could take it. After that episode, I had a few affairs here and there. Then I met Ghislaine Poulain, who worked behind the counter at the post office in Making; she read books and subscribed to the magazine *Growing Old Gracefully*. A brainy public sector worker. We saw each other for years without living together. She cooked for me, I liked that. But I wasn't on my guard: she went and dumped me for someone else as well. A black guy, this one. If she liked them dark, she was well catered for at the post office. Just add a coconut tree at the entrance and you're in the Caribbean. Knocked the stuffing out of me, I can tell you. Didn't see that one coming. I'd picked her because she wasn't very pretty, and she didn't dress so well, but nothing doing. Birds, you just can't trust them. My mum did the same thing to my dad, so it's not like I hadn't been warned.

'Jojo,' I said to myself, 'you're not going to let those birds mess with you ever again.' That was when my hair fell out.

Look, that Arab family from Marseille's come to muscle in on the action. Joined at the hip, that lot. They even do their shopping together. You'd think they were frightened of losing one of them. You can see they're just back from the market. They'll be off again in five minutes. When it's Bin Laden & Co., they're interested, but as soon as it's about a white neighbour who pays his taxes they couldn't care less.

Oh, and guess who's here! Mum and Dad Fournier with their little slut. Back in the day, people used to say: 'son of a bitch'; but with this lot, it's more a case of 'parents of a bitch'. Then again, if I wasn't dead, I'd have held out a year or two 'til she wasn't a minor, because that's not a bad little body she's got on her.

The team from the council's just arrived. Chimpanzees in red, white and blue scarves clearing a solemn path through the crowd. Time was, I served caviar on a silver tray to the mayor who's heading over now. We've got the local elections coming up. If that Commie-voting Soninlaw's dad-in-law makes a big song and dance about people not feeling safe, he'll get in again first round. Oh, and he hasn't forgotten to bring the press along with him. Pulled out all the stops; TV's already here. They pointed their cameras at me while I was being carried off. Under a white sheet, like something out of the Bible.

Yéva, aka Madame Yéva, My Marge or My Old Lady

I'm going to lose my temper in a minute. I've been waiting on this wooden bench for an hour and it's friggin' killing my backside. Commander sweetheart, can't you see you're wasting your time with me? I'm a woman who leads a mind-numbingly ordinary life. I work and then I go back home, every single evening. Like clockwork, I catch the B-train at the same time every day and I see exactly the same faces. I even know which station they'll all get out at. I can't tell you anything about what happened. For the simple reason I know bugger all about it . . . Of course, when someone you know dies, it's a shock. Even if he wasn't exactly my best friend. To tell you the truth, seeing as that's what you're after in your line of work, Morvier was a shit of the first order. I mean, I'm sorry, but the guy really was A SHIT OF THE FIRST ORDER! Yes, it makes me laugh. His death isn't going to change my life, or anyone else's in Making-Ends-Meet. Except I'll have to go further out of my way now, to buy my fags.

Talking of which, d'you mind if I light up? I've been gasping for one for the past hour. Thanks. Anyway, as I was saying, Morvier was a wanker from the old guard, they don't make them like that any more. All right . . . keep your hair on. I get the picture.

I know, commander. No value judgements. You want facts and maybe a piece of my ass too, men generally do . . . Now, you can say you're not interested because you're on duty, but I won't believe you for a second. A few glasses of whisky and Coke and I bet you wouldn't be able to resist. That's how I seduced my husband. I was young and stupid. I thought he was rich and clever. What a fool I was. These days, when I look at him, he reminds me of Buddha, you know the one I mean, the god of those Buddhist people. He's got the same saggy belly and that vacant look too. But the difference is Buddha's busy meditating — it's not the TV that's making him look stupid. Er, sorry, I'm getting off the point. Look, I still don't see what I can do for you . . . You think I can help you find the murderer? Excuse me while I piss myself laughing.

You want me to tell you about my day yesterday? Really? My day? Well . . . it was depressing. Like all the days before it. Maybe even more depressing.

Some days you're better off staying in bed. If I didn't have to scrape together a few extra euros . . . Joseph Frédéric, my boss, was standing by the main entrance, on time for once. So I thought to myself: *What the hell's he doing here?* And before I can say a word he asks me to come and see him in his office at twelve o'clock sharp. No hello. Nothing. It's not like we give each other a peck on the cheek every morning, but this time he was extra cold, the little prick.

I sensed something was up. Sure enough, when I got to my office on the fifth floor, there was one hell of a surprise in store. Sitting on my chair, in my place, was this skinny girl, twenty-five tops, fair hair and posh perfume. That stuff smelt so expensive I knew I'd never be able to afford it. She started off by introducing herself, Sophie Lagarde. Next, she explained in her toffee-nosed voice that she'd be working here on a temporary basis and that she'd been allocated my place. Spoke so proper I nearly had to get my dictionary out. So I told her she didn't need to go to all that effort because I wasn't the one she had to impress and frankly I didn't give a toss what she was called. That was when I realised my belongings weren't there any more. I got the biggest palpitations of my life. I asked her who'd moved them.

When she told me it was two women in their fifties, both well built . . . it wasn't hard for me to guess. Patricia and Simone, of course. What d'you know, I'd been moved off the floor and they'd put me in a corner of the reception area. Sylvie, the obese switchboard operator, was having a great time explaining how the office was being reorganised. From now on, I've got to share that spot with her; I'd just like to point out she weighs nearly a hundred kilos. So, there I am, I'm squeezed right up against the envelopes cupboard. Every time someone needs something, I've got to get up. Which doesn't do much for my scoliosis.

I've noticed you don't have an ashtray, so I hope you don't mind me stubbing this out on the floor. Sorry about the smoke again. You're the sporty type. I can tell.

Now, where was I? Oh yes, so I tried keeping busy until twelve. I could see my life flashing before me, as they say on the telly. I couldn't help thinking of Laurène, this assistant who hanged herself up on the eighth floor last year; she'd been sidelined a few months earlier. It was still taboo to talk about her in the office. *It's my turn now*, I'm thinking. Midday comes around and I go to that dickhead's office. I find out I'll be staying in the corner until I receive new orders.

Joseph Frédéric also explains that I may be required to go up to the fifth floor to train the temp. Train the silly bitch who's pinched my place. Oh, and he might call on me to give the accountants a hand, at the end of the day. That's when I wanted to give him the kind of smack he probably never got as a kid. So, you see, commander sweetheart, if I had the makings of a murderer, I'd have started with Joseph Frédéric. He'd be number one on my list, I can tell you. He looked so smug it made me want to wring his neck, but all I did was sob every last tear in my body in front of that little shit. I've counted and it's been exactly thirteen years since I've cried like that. Not since the day the doctors explained to me, in an office quite like this one, that my son, my baby, was a little bit different from other children. That's what they said back then, probably so as not to upset me: 'different'.

I had all afternoon to digest my humiliation before heading back home. Just like I always do. I walked at the same pace. Same faces in the train carriage. And then that student who always sits opposite me with her five-hundred-page doorstopper, the same book she's been reading since the beginning of term, looked up at me for the first time. 'Excuse me,' she said, 'your mascara's run.' So I glared and told her that if she'd like to get right out of my face I'd be ever so grateful. She dived straight back into her doorstopper. Picked the wrong moment to get on my tits. When I get back home around 7.04 p.m., the first thing I see is Jacko, or Buddha if you prefer. Exactly the same as usual, watching his stupid programme. I ask him what he wants to eat and you'll never guess what he says to me: 'Nothing, I'm not hungry.' You what? Well, of course it's highly unusual, commander. *Nothing, I'm not hungry* . . . Ha-llo, I thought, what's going on here?

In twenty-three years of marriage he's never once said that before. My palpitations started up again. Then he grabbed the remote and switched off the television. The zapper fell to the floor and it made a strange noise because it's covered in bubble wrap stuck on with Sellotape. It's DIY to stop it getting broken, what with my husband being so cack-handed. He's got no balls, commander, even if yesterday he wanted to prove the opposite. I start making a scene, thinking: *This is my chance to let off steam.* But before I know what's happening he's shouting even louder than I am and telling me to shut my fat gob. That I piss him off, and he's had it up to here with my voice, and I've got it com-ing to me, and just because he doesn't work any more doesn't mean he's not a man, and I'm only good for slapping on the make-up and flashing my arse, and if I'm just going to turn my back on him in bed anyway, what's the point ... I'm sparing you the details, commander, I can't begin to tell you how vulgar he was. He even said that if I fancied, I could stuff my turkey escalopes up my you-know-where. I think that's what's called a revolution, commander. Wouldn't you say?

If there was a competition for people who got it in the face, I think I'd have picked up the gold medal yesterday.

And then, to top it all, after his outburst, he put his shoes on and slammed the door, shouting: 'I'm going out for a walk!'

I swear, I didn't know what'd friggin' hit me. I cooked the turkey escalopes, more out of habit than anything. I was on my own. The boys weren't back yet either. So I chomped on my escalopes and fell asleep in my high heels on the couch. Didn't open my eyes again until one o'clock in the morning. That's when I started feeling worried.

What would any mother have done in my place? Yes, I went looking for my child. Yeznig, of course, it goes without saying. Those other two could look after themselves, they know the way home. And anyway, it's not like our place is hard to miss: it's the ugliest of the lot. You caught a glimpse of my baby just now. He's here. Waiting by the drinks machine, that's my little one. Ask the guys in the squad. Sometimes they're nice and bring him back home to me. I know you're finding out how it all works round here. You're over specially for the investigation, aren't you?

Well, because most people know about Yeznig's problem. So I had to go and find him. Normally, I'd send my eldest son, shithead number two; takes after his father. But, as usual, I had to sort the problem out myself. The shutters on the Balto were down, which instantly made me panic. Nearly had organ failure. I was imagining every possible scenario. Especially the worst. I even thought he might have been kidnapped by gypsies. Why gypsies? Well, now you come to mention it . . . That's a good question, commander sweetheart! I'm not really sure. People say funny things about them, you know how it is. In the end, I found him crouched down, chucking up behind the pharmacy in the town centre. I was beside myself with worry. So I asked Yeznig what was wrong, who he was with, what on earth had happened. He just said he was on his own and his tummy hurt. He's a good boy. Life's a bit hard for him, same as it is for everybody. We went back home. When I tucked him up, he told me he wasn't a baby any more, that he was a big boy now. I went to sleep in my own bed, which was empty. No sign of the hubby or Tanièl in the house. I went to work this morning as usual, or nearly. I mean, the same as any Saturday when I'm working. Went back to my place next to fat Sylvie. The day started off normal enough until one of your men from the police station told me the news about Morvier and said I was summoned here in an hour's time. So here I am, commander sweetheart, right in front of you. I know I've already told you this but let me say it again: you really do look the sporty type. I should've married someone like you. A man who wouldn't let himself go. A man who'd have fucking inspired me. Or at least been an inspiring fuck. Is that too much to ask? Anyway, there you go. Please don't thank me. It doesn't help matters. In fact it makes it worse, I'm not used to it.

But I'll tell you what, commander sweetheart, if you could call that shit Joseph Frédéric and explain why I've been out of the office this afternoon, I'd be ever so grateful. The dickhead might just screw me over again and deduct this from my wages.

Tanièl, aka Tani, Turkey Boy or Lazy Bugger

First off, I thought this was about the attack on Mr Leroy, but then I reckoned: 'Nah, it's my beef with Ali Chacal. Mr Leroy dropped the charges . . . ' I was sweating it when you rang our house. It's lucky I was in for once. Did you call my college first? Oh, so you know I don't go there any more? OK, I guess we've said it now.

To be honest with you, sir, I never imagined anything like this happening. I thought you only got to see this kind of stuff on TV. I mean, it's totally mad. Yeah. This story wilds me out. You're gonna have a nightmare arresting the killer. Why? Because nobody liked the guy, end of. Nobody'll miss him, you get me? I know you're not supposed to say shit like that, what with him being dead and everything, but it's bare true, innit? At least you get the picture. Even if you go all out, you won't find anyone who liked him. The man, yeah, he didn't have no family, no friends, no hair . . . Just kidding. It's OK, sir, I was kidding. What? Even that, you're going to type it into the computer? Shit.

Oh shit. What, even when I said 'shit'? All right, I'll stop talking crap.

I've just run into my mum outside and she's waiting to explode, big time. I hope you didn't say anything to her about me bunking off college? I know what she's like. If she finds out she'll go apeshit, man.

I told my parents about the time I merked our Head of Year. I wanted to play the model son, honest and all that bull . . . But forget it, you should've seen how they reacted. They already treated me like I was worthless, specially my Marge, but it got a thousand times worse after that. On the one, she was bad-mouthing me even more than before. On the two, she goes and bins all my rap CDs. Like it's the rappers' fault our life's such a pile of shit. It's got nothing to do with them. And it's not like she'll be any less stupid when she goes to bed at night, just because she's chucked out her Aznavour records; that's not going to solve her problems.

Everything gets blown out of proportion with her. I bet even you'd had enough after she'd been in here. You can tell me, I'm used to it. Anyhow, that's why I decided to keep my mouth shut from now on. I just said to myself: 'It's over.'

As far as Joël goes, I'm planning on telling

you everything. I don't want to lie, I'm guessing you know I was over there yesterday.

So here goes. I woke up at seven o'clock, grabbed my empty bag and headed out, like I do every morning. I was sitting outside with my boys from the estate. Same journey I make every morning. My usual, you get me. I like them; we catch some serious jokes together. Seeing how it was cold and all that, we didn't stay outside for long. We went up to Nasser's place, he's this guy from the endz, his dad's dead and his mum's a hospital cleaner. There was no one home. We chilled and played on the Xbox till about one or two o'clock.

I couldn't really say, to be honest. I know it was around then . . . but I can't remember, sir, if it was more like one o'clock or two o'clock . . . I can tell you ain't a gamer, or you'd know about losing track of time. Plus, I ain't lucky enough to have a nice chrome watch like yours to check it on, you get me? So, what make is it? No kidding, it's OVA-NICE, man. Yeah, well, I like cool gear, not that I've got much. It's been 'no' for 'nuff years. I reckon my first word as a baby was 'bill' or 'overdue payment' . . . What d'you expect? We weren't allowed nothing. 'Specially me. No holidays. No presents. No Christmas. No birthdays.

Any money left over was for my brother. For Yeznig's doctors, for Yeznig's games, for Yeznig's holidays. I'll tell you what, those group holidays for the disabled, they're the real deal. I just stayed inside all summer. Don't get me wrong, I love Yeznig, he's my little bro. But sometimes I fancy being in his shoes. I guess you're thinking that's an awful thing to say, but you know what . . . it's true. I used to want to be disabled. When I was a kid, I tried talking a bit like him so my old lady would pay me some attention, but all she did was call me a spaz. That's when I started chilling with my boys outside. Hardly ever came home any more. It's so you understand why outside is like a reflex, for me.

So we left Nasser's place. I trashed everyone at football, same as I always do, and they were pissed off. I even told Nasser that one day his Xbox was going to make a formal complaint about me being such a powerful gamer.

Then I left them and went to find Ali on his way out of college. The cunt didn't have no lessons that afternoon. Sorry, no, really, I just can't help insulting him. He used to be my blud. But yesterday he ova-betrayed me. I swear. It was well out of order. I always used to stick up for him when my Marge bad-mouthed him. But my old lady was right all along. She never had a good feeling about him. Said he was a bad influence on me. At the end of the day, she's right. He led me on, getting me into so much beef, and all along he was toeing the line. For one thing, he always went to college and he even got a special mention from the teachers after his first term. But I was a stupid drop-out. Nice one, Tani.

Anyhow, I'll get on with it. If we went to the Balto, it wasn't for the vibe, or clearly we'd have gone to the Champs-Elysées any day. But it's such a hassle getting out of this place, we don't even bother no more. So there was Joël, with his big fat bald patch — I can see why my dad calls him 'The Rink'. He was up for flaunting it again. As soon as we get there, he comes over all aggressive. Like: 'What the hell are you doing here, you pair of good-for-nothings? Why aren't you in the doghouse?' And some other bull I can't remember . . . Well, what does he think? It's not like we were there to catch up on his news. He's always dissing his customers. Ali and me wanted to merk him, for real. Then we felt sorry for him because he was old. I mean, soon as we go into his stinking bar he wants to try it on. Lucky for him it was us — we don't beat up old men. So we sat down and had a drink. I had a bit of money on me.

How come? 'Low it, man, I don't have to tell you, it's nothing to do with this business. Er . . . no, I'm not looking for trouble, sir. Look, it's nothing dodgy. It's just my girl Magalie who sorts me out from time to time. She helps me out because she knows I'm skint. It's my old lady's fault, she collects my EMA at the start of the year — my education maintenance allowance, you get me — and I'm left with zip. Not a cent. She doesn't give me nothing. My old lady reckons I ain't got no outgoings at my age, coz there's everything we need at home. Yeah right. It's a good thing my boys lend me stuff from time to time. When I yell at her for my cash, she says she's putting it towards the mortgage, and that when she and Dad croak it this friggin' house — as she calls it — will belong to me. I get it, so, like, it's all for me at the end of the day, for later on, for my own good. I've had it with grown-ups frying my head. It was the same at school. How can they know what's good for me when they don't even know who I am? Whatever. I don't really know where Magalie gets the papers from. I'm guessing she bums them off her parents. I know she tells her old lady she'll leave home unless she gets everything she wants. And it works. Mine would just say bugger off, good riddance.

So we had a drink, yeah, and we were kind of zoned. That's what alcohol does to you. I guess you know about that. Yeah. I mean, no, not in that way. I'm not insinuating nothing. Everybody knows about the effects of alcohol, that's what I mean. I don't need to go into detail. It was mainly Ali, who's not used to getting pissed. It got to the point when we had no idea what time it was any more. We were having a right laugh. Messing about. I can't even remember what bull we were telling each other. We must've looked like wastemans. And then I remembered poor Magalie — I'd totally zapped her from my mind. So I told Ali, and that's when it all started going pear-shaped. He went: 'Whatever, who gives a shit, that bucket pussy can wait for us!' My head was pounding when I heard him say that. And then he goes: 'I've already banged her bare times behind your back.' That's when there's no stopping me. Even if I work on it, it's a big problem for me. It's got to come out. I'm right on the edge, man. Sometimes I want to smash everything. I can't help it.

I insulted his whole family and I had him by the nose. Baldie, I mean Joël, got us by the scruff of our necks and marched us outside. He told us to deal with it off the premises or he'd call the po-pos. He even told Ali they'd send him back to where he came from. Don't arks me why he needed to throw in a stupid remark like that.

So I beat him up in front of the Balto. Nobody moved. Bunch of wimps. The old codgers propping up the bar watched us going for it. They looked like they were having a good time. After a few minutes, the baker's sons, Junior and Pascal, or the Baguette Brothers as we call them round here, came over to separate us. And then I split. I know it was just talk. My girl'd never do anything with Ali Chacal. She's too good-looking for him. Like a true blud, I'd been planning to take Ali over there with me. Well — round her place, of course! There was going be a vibe going down. A party, you get me? She'd organised a Tektonik night. So, OK, me and my crew are more into rap. Call us crazy but we don't really get those Tecktonik guys. Their trousers are too tight and they go all out with the hair gel. You'd think their mums gave birth to them like that. But it's not like they invented anything new with those haircuts. If you arks me, they already had the same ones in *Dragon Ball Z* ten years ago. Anyhow, you could bet there'd be plenty of blondes from de Beauvoir College at the party, plus their fit-looking cousins. So Ali was in with a chance of linking with a wifey. Plus, it was going to be a laugh. I'd even got a laxative in my jacket pocket to put in Perno's food — that's Magalie's dad's mutt. My personal revenge on her old man. I wanted it to be a surprise for that stupid fat racist who always takes me for a fuckin' gypsy.

I mashed Ali nice and good. When I do something, I do it proper. You're a policeman, sir. You understand about honour and all that. Or how's it gonna look? Like I'm a neek, for real. A neek? Well, it's like someone who ain't got no backbone, you get me? I guess that's what it means.

Afterwards, I decided to pass by my place. I was on my way when I got the message on my mobile. It was my girl. Her text was jarrin'. Last thing I needed was her adding to my troubles. So she gives me all this big drama about how she's going to 'leave me' and then she ends her bloody message with THE million-euro threat. Like her period's late or whatever. Now, I just have to hear the word 'period' and I'm in a panic. It's not my thing, I don't get any of that girl stuff and I don't want to either. So, it's like maybe she's pregnant. I was wilding out. And she said in her text she'd be at the Balto.

Dunno when exactly but it must've been at least six o'clock when I got back home. It wasn't like I'd taken a hammering, but I'd still got this cut above my eye. There was loads of blood so it looked kind of scary, but to be honest, compared with what I did to him, it was no big deal. I let myself in through the back door. Nice and quiet. My dad saw me. He faked being interested in me for about two seconds. Arksed me where I was going, I think, and that was it. I reckon he didn't even notice I was bleeding. I went into the bedroom and my little bro Yeznig was sat in there. He was already back from HUW, the centre where he volunteers.

He was drawing circles on a sheet of paper. It's another of his weird habits. He draws these red circles. Loads of them. We don't know what to do with all his circles. He won't let us throw them away. It's cute because he saw my face was bruk-up, so he went off to find some 'red', from his first-aid kit. That's what he calls Mercurochrome. He was playing at being doctor and he stuck a kid's plaster on my face, with animal pictures. I couldn't help it, I bawled, my nerves were shot to pieces. Hate it when that happens. Plus my little bro saw me. I didn't want him being upset, or grassing me up to my parents. So I jetted.

Faster than the speed of light. A guy who's angry don't hang around. I was so nervous I almost ran to get there. You think someone'd shoved a stick of dynamite down my Calvin's.

I spotted her from a hundred metres off. She was wearing all pink. Talk about feeling *this* embarrassed. Dunno what she was trying to look like, but if it was candyfloss she'd hit the jackpot. She arksed if we could go and sit down. I was bricking it about going back into the bar, but seeing how she didn't know I'd been in a fight, I didn't say anything. We went in. The Rink couldn't resist.

'If you're looking for your cage we're not the zoo here.' Worst is, there's always some wanker who laughs at his jokes.

Magalie arksed me why he said that. So I was like: 'You know what a dickhead he is.' She let it go. I was trying to stay calm, which wasn't easy. And then she goes and arks a stupid question, like she does sometimes. She arks me if I think she looks a bit like Paris Hilton, dressed like that . . . I was so pissed off. I wanted to tell her she looked like Barbie's cousin, but I just went: 'I don't give a shit! Are you pregnant or what?'

Sorry, sir, I don't mean to offend you, but you can't waste time in a situation like that. She showed me this long plastic stick that looked sort of like a digital thermometer. On one side, there was this question mark. So she shows me this square screen all lit up in pink,

72

and it says PREGNANT. 'It's the latest pregnancy test on the market. Ninety-nine point nine per cent accurate. Here, read this if you like.'

I peed my pants when she said that, three drops of piss. No, my old lady doesn't know about this either. I ain't even going there. It'd be worse than the palpitations she gets. So I told my girl to get a move on, to clear up her fucking test and stash it somewhere. The main thing was to stop her telling anybody. We had to think tactics. To give myself a bit of time, I said I wouldn't go to her Tektonik party and we'd see each other later. She made a face. She didn't seem to realise how much shit we were in. She paid for our drinks and I watched her leave. I could see Magalie shaking her ass on the way out and I was thinking: 'Fuck, that wifey's gonna have my baby.' And all of a sudden, I didn't feel like going back home. No way. The last thing I wanted to do was run into my mum. I couldn't have dealt with it, for real. So I started walking towards the estate. It's like a reflex, with me. That's when I noticed a familiar figure, this flabby shape heading my way in the dark. I swear, I nearly fainted. I think I must've pissed myself a few drops more. It was my old man. For one thing, it was *this* weird seeing him upright. Plus, he

73

was walking. We'd all started to wonder if his engine hadn't rusted up from being stuck to the couch for so long. I decided to whistle to him. He didn't hear me. Thing is, he's deaf if you don't talk right in front of him. So I went over and grabbed him by his tracksuit sleeve. He was scared as a kid. Straight up, he was shaking all over. 'I've got nothing on me! Don't hurt me!' Poor guy didn't even recognise me. Must've thought I was a hoodie who wanted to knife him, or something. I guess I called out: 'Dad, it's me!' to calm him down. Too much TV on the brain. In the end he made it back to Planet Earth and arksed me what I was doing there. I fired the same question straight back. It was more weird him being out at that kind of time. Next thing, he's telling me he nearly climbed into one of the caravans behind the station, to get some satisfaction. He meant the prostitutes. I looked at him, he was trembling — it freaked me out. I've never seen my old man like that. He said it had to stay between the two of us.

So we went and ran round the park a couple of times. You probably think it's stupid, but he used to make us do that when we were younger, me and my little bro, if we were all worked up. So I said to him: 'D'you remember, Dad, when you used to make us go for a run, to stop us getting into trouble?'

And he went: 'Those were the good old days. We don't talk to each other any more. We never talk to each other. You're my boy, after all. We should have a chat more often.'

It was spooky he'd picked that evening for a father-son chat, as in: 'Sonny, let me tell you about life.' It wasn't like I'd got any good news for him.

When he seemed a bit more chilled, I told him about Magalie. It was a nightmare trying to spit it out. Poor Jacko, he couldn't get over it.

He looked me straight in the eye and said: 'We should get some sleep. Let's talk about this tomorrow. And we'll have a chat about college too.'

That's when I clocked he knew but hadn't said anything.

Me and the old man got back at dawn, we were dead beat. That's everything, sir. After that, I went to bed next to my little bro and fell asleep.

Jacques, aka Jacko, the Old Man or Hubby

It's been a long time since someone sat down opposite me to hear what I've got to say. A story like this, it's more the kind of thing you watch in the murder-mystery slot, Thursday nights. Love those TV series. Mainly *Julie Lescaut*. If you've got one like her in your squad, don't forget to introduce me. Good-looking woman. Gentle. Not vulgar. Someone you know you could count on.

What I did yesterday? Oh . . . nothing special. If it's unusual stories you're after, don't look here.

Yesterday morning, I woke up with bellyache. Didn't take a shower. Sometimes I just don't feel like it, you know. I hardly ever leave the house, so I might as well save on water. My way of helping pay the mortgage. Same goes for flushing. I'm not being dirty. It's just about making ends meet. I watched *General Hospital* while I drank my coffee and ate some of yesterday's bread. I was waiting for *Melrose Place*. There was another letter from Tanièl's college in the post. I just read them and bin them. Yup, that's all. Of course that's all. You must think I've got no balls. I know. But saying nothing doesn't make you a wuss. Marcel, our boss at the factory, used to say: 'If what you've got to say isn't as beautiful as silence, then keep quiet.'

After the incident with his Head of Year, I thought Tanièl would calm down a bit, but that kid's so hard-headed, skull like a stone. I feel bad about it now. If I'd been more involved in bringing them up, we wouldn't be in this position. I let her choose everything. Even their names. She wanted ones from her country. Seemed odd to me, but I didn't say anything. She's decided everything in our life. All of yesterday, I kept getting these flashbacks and it's nuts how they were all the same. Yéva standing there, thighs out for all to see, waggling her fake nails under my nose. Calling me a bloody idiot in front of the kids. She'd always end with: 'You can't say anything, lard arse!' She took all the decisions. Except for the house, I was the one who found it. She's trampled all over my face with those high heels of hers, I've been crushed for twenty years, but last night, while I was watching *Everybody's Talking About it*, I decided things were going to change.

That was when I saw my sonny walking past. I was surprised to see him home so early. 'Where've you been?' I asked him. I clocked the state his face was in. Not a pretty sight but I didn't press him on it. The kid probably thought I hadn't even noticed, as usual. But I realised he'd been in a fight. Not even ten minutes later, I see him heading out again like a thief. 'So,' I go, 'where are you off to now?' 'Nowhere,' he says. Before he's out the door, I add: 'Lucky you're too old, or I'd have got Super Nanny round!' He didn't even bother answering, poor kid.

Must seem ridiculous to you, but what kind of advice can an unemployed man like me, stuck in front of the telly all day, give his boy?

Haven't felt like a man in a long time now. Just something pointless dumped on the couch.

At least, if I can be useful for your investigation . . .

Oh, the winning ticket? Yes, I found out about that yesterday. It was all part of me coming to my senses, I can tell you! Who told you about it? Confidential . . . Yeah right . . . Everyone must know about it by now. Marcel rang the doorbell. Some days, when he doesn't see me at the Balto, he brings my scratch-cards to the house. He's the real deal, Marcel. He'll never drop me.

I noticed he didn't seem so good. When I asked him if there was a problem, he told me to concentrate on what I was scratching. 'Marcel,' I go, 'if you're talking to me like that it means you know something.' So then he says how the Black Widow told him that the fifteen thousand euros for the Balto's new facelift . . . well, that was my loot! She'd seen him rescue my Banco ticket. Mine. Bloody good bloke, that Marcel. I've known him thirty-four years, and he's as honest as they come. He was always straight with his workers at the factory too.

So why didn't that fruitcake widow say so before? I can't prove anything now. What could I do? Smash Jojo's jaw in? And then what?

It wouldn't have made any difference. Plus he had a gun, did the Rink. So it's not like I'd have stood a chance trying to get the better of him.

I haven't been in a fight for years. My hands are only good for switching channels. In fact, my lady wife always has a go at me for not leaping to her defence when some bloke's getting on her nerves. Talk's cheap! All she needs to do is wear longer skirts. You've got to accept when you're getting old, that's what I say. Respect the rules of the game. If you flounce around half naked, people stare at you. That's just how it is. I know I do, for one. Don't you?

This is just between the two of us, captain
. . . you can tell me. Don't you ever find
yourself eyeing up the dolly birds? Of course
you do! Just like everyone else. Right, got you
. . . Like you say, let's stick to the subject . . .

I didn't say a word. Didn't budge either.
With a motive like that, I'm the ideal culprit.
I know. But let's be realistic here, I wouldn't
have had the balls.

All I did, while I was waiting for Yéva to get
back from work, was pull up a few weeds in
the garden and watch part two of *Everyone's
Talking About It.*

The topic was: 'Learning to say No'.

And you know what, there are plenty of
people like me. People who put up and shut
up. Who take it lying down. Shit, why not say
it, who haven't got much personality. Because
deep down that's the problem. At least I
know I'm not alone. And out of all those
people, there are plenty who decide to rebel
from one day to the next. They suddenly say
STOP.

If I'm honest with you, I'd been getting a
bit worked up all by myself. So when I heard
her heels clacking on the tiles, I shot out of
my seat like a cork. I'd been bottling up too
much inside. I told her a few home truths.
You should've seen me go for it. She didn't
know what'd hit her.

Then I got the hell out. After all, it's partly because of her I've done bugger all on this earth. I've brought some kids into the world, but anyone can do that. I say that because my boy's just told me about this dopey cow he's been seeing for a few months, and now he's gone and got her pregnant by mistake. I mean, can you imagine? I'll have seen everything. Haven't even had time to be a dad and now I'm going to be a grandad. Seventeen years old, my boy. What a generation! But what I want to know is how he managed it. Did he send the sperm by text message or what?

So, yes, like you say, getting back to what happened. I had a blazing row with Yéva. I didn't really know where I was going, and then I had the idea of paying a visit to the prostitutes. For the first time, mind.

I was heading for the caravans, but before I got there I met Tanièl, my sonny. We went running in the park, it did me the power of good. We chatted a bit and then we went home. There you go, captain. Nothing else.

Nadia and Ali Chacal, aka the Twins, the Marseille Posse or the Jackals

— Can I start, colonel?

— You're always the one who starts —

— Shut it! I'd rather go first than let you come out with all your rubbish.

— Yeah, right, whatever, go for it, Miss Brainbox.

— Well. Hmm. First of all, colonel, I'd like to point out this is the first time we've had anything to do with the police in our family. I mean, except for my father who got beaten up a long time ago, but that's just what happened back then . . . Secondly, as far as this case is concerned, none of us went to the Balto that day, apart from my brother Ali who's sitting next to me. My father boycotts it. He wasn't made to feel welcome there. At least, not the way he deserves.

— Pfff . . .

— What do you mean, pfff? It's the truth. So anyway, before it's Ali's turn to speak, I just wanted to say that, for once, the violence and barbaric stuff is going down on your turf.

Well, that's it. No flies on us. It's our turn to be the spectators now, to watch, to give the running commentary, to say: *Oooh, dearie me, those Frenchies are so barbaric. I have to say, those French country bumpkins really are very strange.* It makes a change to hear about a crime story that's got nothing to do with the *banlieue* or immigration. Usually, apart from road accidents, there's always a link, even if it's a subtle one.

— I don't believe it, will you stop giving us this crap? Honestly, colonel, I'm sorry about my sister. It's my turn now because, if you don't watch out, she'll take you on a tour of the whole souk while she's at it. When I talk, I'm not bitter. Nadia carries too much of our parents' baggage around with her. And you know what, that suitcase weighs seven hundred kilos. I've got rid of mine. It's true that we hadn't known Joël for long but, at the end of the day, Nadia's not far off when she calls him a racist.

— At the end of the day . . . ? That expression makes me laugh. At the end of the day! Why just at the end of the day? He was a racist any time of day, in the morning, in the afternoon, whatever time of day you fancy . . . That guy sweated racism out of every pore, he slopped it on like aftershave.

— Look, it happens. It's like being deaf, or

blind, or getting cancer. Racism's a disease, that's all. Everyone has a right to their own opinions. So, I was going to the Balto with a friend —

— What d'you mean, a friend? Someone who smashes your face in is still a friend? For one thing, he's more of a rival. They're in love with the same girl, who's just a fat bitch.

— Man, you're so full of it! 'Low it! Have you swallowed Skyrock FM whole or what? You don't give up, do you? Where was I? Oh yeah. So on the Rink's last day I did go and have a few drinks with my friend, Turkey Boy. He's called Tanièl actually. Turkey Boy's just a nickname to wind him up . . . He's *so* not into it, but it's not like we mean any harm. Down South, we mess around a lot — it's a sport in Marseille. But we're short on sunshine up here, along with the sense of humour that goes with it. So we were together and then he was meant to see Magalie, this girl I LIKE as well. You're a man, you'll understand. I was trying to distract him, make him forget his date. I was sure it was just a question of time for Magalie and me. I was working out my plan, nice and steady. Basically, we drank bare: I got smashed and so did he, but a bit less. You know how it is, I said something he took the wrong way and bam, it flared right up, we got into a fight. It happened around —

— Around six thirty.

— How d'you know?

— Well, I saw what time it was when you got back, and I just subtracted that from the time it takes to get home from town, and bingo.

— So anyway, I went back home afterwards. No idea how, by the way. Oh yeah. The Baguette Brothers gave me a lift in their wib. They've got this weird car, with tattoos and a neon light on top and all those gizmos. They're into souping it up. Makes me laugh. I felt a bit queasy after that, so I'm not really sure . . .

— Let me refresh your memory. I've got all the details, colonel. I'd got back from college an hour earlier. I'd had time to do my science homework, peel the vegetables for the *chorba* mum was cooking, fold up the clean clothes and put them away in the wardrobe my three little sisters use. All that while Ali was hosing himself down with beer and fighting with his rival, the Turk. We're so different it's crazy, when you think how we inherited the same genes. But there you go.

My brother's always ending up in fixes. Ever since he was a kid. And I'm the one who has to cover for him. You don't know what Arab mums are like, but I'm telling you it's

85

best to avoid getting into a mess like that. Luckily, my little sisters were in their bedroom brushing their Barbies' hair. They didn't hear a thing.

Ali — the only boy in the family can I just say — comes back home with a bleeding nose and it's like his brain's checked out. He couldn't even stand up any more. My mother was screaming hysterically and starting to panic. So then Dad only goes and wakes up. Now if you're going to disturb Dad while he's taking a nap or watching the news, there'd better be a good reason for it. I suppose you could say that was the case here. I got Ali to sit down on a kitchen chair and I cleaned him up with Betadine. He looked hideous. Plus his breath stank. The works.

My parents were shouting at him in Kabyle, they were asking loads of questions. But all he would say was: 'Talk in French, please, I don't understand a word, my head's killing me.'

At that point, I swear to you that if Ali hadn't been his only son, my father would've kicked him out. We're straight up kind of people.

Instead, he asked my mother to warm up some milk for Ali and told me to put some ice on his head. Then he went to lie down again, leaving 'we'll deal with this later' hanging in the air.

My father's got this look in his eye when he's angry . . . there's too much going on inside, you really don't want to cross him.

— All right! OK! We've got the picture. I know I went to sleep after the glass of warm milk.

— Yeah, *you* fell asleep. It's all right for some. You're not the one who had to listen to mum's yada-yada for the next hour. 'And *this* . . . and *that* . . . and *why* in God's name . . . ? We're living like paupers here in France, but it's for you children . . . We've made so many sacrifices for you . . . We didn't have anything, not even shoes . . . We lived through the war . . . And blah blah blah . . . You're so ungrateful . . . ' The usual hit list. I've got too many rants like that stashed away in my head. Even at school, I put myself under pressure. I'm always thinking: if I mess up my life, I'm messing up their lives too.

It simmers away in my brain. But Ali can let go of it, the seven hundred kilos, like he said. There's nothing inside his head, just water.

— D'you think you're at the shrink's or something? This is a police station. Don't take any notice of her, colonel. That's all there is to know. Nothing else. We've got no connection with Joël's death. There's nothing

87

important about what we've been telling you. It's just details.

— Too right. Tiny details, even more trivial than the place we and our parents occupy in this country. That's it. There's nothing else to add.

Magalie Fournier, aka the Blonde, the Slut or Turkey Boy's Wifey

I know. I understand, but I still don't see what I've got to do with any of this. Because if you're talking to everyone who goes to the Balto . . . you'll see some real *space cookies* turning up in this room. LOL.

Look, basically Joël's someone I've never liked. He was always watching me out of the corner of his eye and staring at my butt. That and telling my dad about my every move, whenever he got the chance. It's how my old man found out about me and Tani. I mean, what business was it of his? Always sticking his nose in where it wasn't wanted. I bet he's still bugging the shit out of everybody wherever he is now.

It's just . . . Sorry, this isn't to do with it, but what star sign are you, officer?

Of course it matters, that's why I'm asking you. LOL. What? OMG, you don't know your sign? How can you leave home without reading your horoscope? Whatever, too bad, just give me your date of birth, I'll work it out myself. Come on . . . you know you want

to really, it's no big deal . . . ah . . . 27 July
. . . You're a Leo! Wow! I love fire signs. Nice
temperament. LOL. Now I feel like cooperat-
ing with you. ROFL. Just kidding.

OK, so . . . As I was saying, that's how my
pops knew about Tanièl and me. He calls
him 'the gypsy' or 'that pikey'. It drives me *so*
crazy. The guy's a loser. He's soooo borr-ring,
there's like an intergalactic hole where his life
should be. As for my *mom*, don't even go
there . . .

Yeah, I watch a lot of American TV, I guess
it shows. Cool, hey, officer? Gotta get with
the times. And seeing as Mr Witter, my
English teacher, fancies me big time, he gives
me all these extra lessons. All my girlfriends
at college say he'd *die* for me. They make out
he drools when he's looking at me . . . It
wouldn't surprise me. You can tell he's, like,
totally into me. LOL. So I'm trying to get my
English perfect because, later on, I want to
travel. America mainly, that's my goal. You
can't become somebody here, you'll be a
nobody and you'll stay that way for the rest
of your life. The proof: my mum and dad,
I've got a big sister called Virginie. She's
drop-dead gorgeous — bet you'd like her, by
the way. When she'd had enough, she cleared
out and moved to Paris. Well, I'd beat that:
I'd go to Los Angeles, California, United

States of America. Sure, Tani would follow me over there. Anyway, it's not like I'm worried or anything, I'll find someone better between now and then. LOL.

What? Well, it's true. You've always got to find someone who's as cool as you are. It's what guys do already. As soon as they buy a new car, they find the girl who matches it.

I've got a clear head when it comes to these things. It's in my birth chart. That's the way it is.

Where was I ... ? Yesterday, I finished classes at five o'clock. I've brought you a photocopy of my timetable to save you time. LOL. It was my mum's idea. I actually listened to her for once, but the poor old bag was dosed up to the eyeballs. She's going to be *this* happy for the next few days, making out she's got her authority back. FYI, I'm sorry but, like, I don't see how she can get it back when she never had any in the first place ... Anyway, enough with the detail, let's move on. So, it didn't seem like there was anything different about that day. I had more guys from college asking me out. Plus more jealous looks from Nadia Chacal. She's one of the ugliest girls I know. Poor thing. I dazzle her: when she walks past me, she closes her eyes.

Tani was meant to meet me after lessons,

because that evening there was going be this Tektonik party round at mine. I'd bought myself a Paris Hilton outfit. Saw it in *Life Star* magazine. It gives contact details for where to get the same garms as all my favourite stars, but cheaper. It totally suited me. All pink. Pastel colours are on trend this year. And that's a tip-off.

By six thirty there was still no sign of Tani. I asked Karine Z if she wanted to wait with me; she always hangs around college before heading back home. She said OK. Waiting on your own means you're, like, such a *loser*, it's for people like Nadia Chacal.

So anyway, if Karine had said no, I'd have set all the guys from college against her the next day; obviously they'd have been on my side, they're all drooling over me. Or I'd have found someone else to chill with. At college, people are fighting over who gets to hang out with me or sit at my table in the canteen. LOL.

Yeah, you could say everyone likes me. No shame in admitting it. Proof: I've got a hundred and eighty-seven *friends* on MSN. As soon as one of them bugs me, I delete them and add another. It's not so difficult getting into the circle of my MSN contacts, it's more staying there that's not *easy*.

So what I'm saying is: half an hour later

there's still no Tani in the zone. See what I mean about listening to your horoscope? They said it. I'm Virgo and when Virgo's moon's in Pluto, it's a bad sign. I'm not the kind of babe you keep waiting, I thought that was clear in his little head.

Karine Z's telling me about her life and I'm thinking: *Well, I guess this is one way of making time pass.* She's talking about one of her ten guys. I'm like: how does she do it, not getting caught when she's dating so many guys, all at once? What with this town being so small and everything. In Los Angeles, fine, no problem, but everybody knows everybody in Making-Ends-Meet. So, all of a sudden Karine Z gets something out of her handbag and signals for me to move in close. You'll never guess what she shoves in my face: a big fat positive pregnancy test. 'I just did this in the bogs,' she goes. 'You piss on it. It's the latest pregnancy test on the market. Ninety-nine point nine per cent accurate.' And written in capital letters on a pink screen you've got: PREGNANT. Scoop of the century. You should've seen that silly bitch's face. LOL. She made me promise not to tell anyone. I told her not to worry and that she'd be better off handing the test over to me to take home, or else her parents might find it. It'd be totally safe round at mine, my folks know they're officially banned from coming into my room. They wouldn't even clock if I had a stark-naked guy hiding in my wardrobe. They're totally out of it.

That's when I sent Tani the famous text. Killer SMS. I can read it to you, I didn't delete it, it's still in my drafts because it's a classic. 'Itz all ova, u screw up 2 much, Im not yr bitch, ysdiw8, u know 0 xcpt carpk, find anuva chik. PS. Reds bare 18 . . . b scared, b v scared. Going 2 Balto 2nite. M8 me 4 121. DNBL8. Top prio8Y.' I really went for it. LOL.

At least after that I knew he'd turn up. I dropped by Karine Z's place to pick up the iPod I'd lent her, I needed it for the party, it's got the best Tektonik tracks on it. She made me promise all over again to keep her secret, which of course I did, LOL. Then she stayed home, seeing how she wasn't invited to my bash, and I headed for the Balto as planned.

I saw Tani jetting over there. He was running so fast his trainers were gouging out the grass. He looked like a tennis star, with his red basketball cap jammed on his head. It was dead cute. I could see him coming towards me and I just kept saying to myself: 'Don't laugh.'

It was really hard not to, it was going to be *so* comic. LMHO. Or even LMAO. Ah

. . . you're not following me, officer . . . I get it, you're a bit like my parents, aka the generation that read books in front of log fires, nights out at the disco and all that. OK, so LMHO means 'laughing my head off' and LMAO is nearly the max, it's 'laughing my ass off'. There's also LSHITIPAL, which means 'laughing so hard I think I peed a little'. But you should use that one sparingly, like only when you've got a really bad fit of the giggles, otherwise it loses its value. D'you get the picture now? When you're chatting online, you can't see each other, you're not face to face, so they're like codes to tell the person you're communicating with how you're feeling, like when it's *funny* . . . There's even little icons, you know, *smileys* . . .

Yeah, yeah, you're right, we're getting away from the subject. And I was, like, at the cliffhanger in my story.

So, we went into the bar and sat down. Joël made some kind of weird remark, I don't really remember what. He used to make so many stupid comments, that jerk. I was surprised he didn't make one about my outfit for once. He got such a kick out of doing that. He'd always be inspecting me. As in: 'Why don't you just take that skirt right off, it's not hiding anything, in fact it's not a skirt at all, it's a handkerchief! You're looking like a right slut today; if I was your dad, things'd be very different . . . ' So then I'd tell him he wasn't my dad and that I'd dress the way I liked, so there. You could tell he didn't have any friends because he had all this time to hang around me. Or else he must've been another one who was *so* in love with me, that disgusting old pervert.

Long story short, Tani and me went to sit at the back of the bar. I tried getting him to relax at first, I made a bit of small talk . . . chatted about me . . . but he was too stressed, so it just bugged him even more. He totally wanted to know if I was pregnant. He asked me, straight up. That was when, for the first time in my life, I realised I'd make a great actress. I was looking him straight in the eye as I rummaged around in my bag, then I got out the test. LOL. Should've seen the face he pulled, poor guy. It was, like, so diddy. To start with, he didn't get it. He bent his head over to read what was written on it. Then he looked at me like he was waiting for an explanation. That's when I pulled out *the* killer sentence, trying to remember what Karine Z had said. 'It's the latest pregnancy test on the market. Ninety-nine point nine per cent accurate. Here, read this if you want to find out more.'

Straight out of a film. Thanks, Karine Z,

for being pregnant that day. I owe you, big time.

I thought he'd at least come to my party after a round of electric shock treatment like that, but no, Mister needed to think it all over.

What kind of a question's that? Course I'm going to tell him the pregnancy thing's a hoax. I'm sure he'll be cool about it, he loves me to bits. That guy would kill for me, he's mad for me. And anyway, I did it to make him understand he's got to deserve me. You've got to deserve a girl with ratings like mine. He'll never keep me waiting again.

Yeah, OK, so I was kind of in a strop. I felt let down about going home alone, without him, without my Tani. Plus he was all shaken up. I headed off, after paying for our drinks like usual, LOL. If I had a rear-view mirror on my body, I'd have got a buzz off seeing his face. But I couldn't turn round. If I'd done that, I'd have broken one of my golden rules. In issue 97 of *HC* magazine — *Hot & Cute* — there was this cool article I'd cut out and stuck to my wall, near the photos of me at the beach. It was called 'Your Golden Rules for Staying Irresistible'. In at number 3 was NEVER, EVER (in red ink) turn round when you leave at the end of a date. If you do, you're a loser because it takes away all your mystery and charm. The idea's to walk away like a princess, trailing a sweet scent behind you, and to head off like you mean business while gently wiggling your butt. I pulled out all the stops. And WOW . . . I've got to say, it really does work.

So in the end I sent a group message on MSN to cancel the party, which must've left the ones I'd invited for the first time broken-hearted. In the subject heading, I put: 'BION the party's cancelled'.

At least I knew I'd get some peace and quiet. My parents were away. Making out they were feeling really 'tense'. Because of me, supposedly. Like I'm going to feel sorry for them. It's thanks to those two rejects I don't get to see my big sister any more. I spent the evening on my own like a no-hoper, Nadia Chacal style. I watched TV and went to bed. But I didn't forget to take my pill, you never know . . .

Yeznig, aka Baby, Fatty or the Spaz

For me, there'd be three people here. But for Tani and Mummy, only one. Just the man, that's you with the grey hair. Who are you, the lady with the glasses, and you, mister?

I knew it Psychiatrists. You'll all look the same. I don't like them, those psychiatrists. Since I'll be a very small child, I'll go to see psychiatrists and they'll be mean and nasty. They said things about me I wouldn't want to hear. That's it.

I'll be sad that Joël is dead. I'll have cried. Even if I know he's dead, so he wasn't going to cry for me.

It's always sad to die. He was never going to have a baby. One day, Joël said there are countries where they kill babies who'll be born like me. Handicapped. With strange things in their heads. They're not allowed to live.

I was going to work at HUW. Arnaud won't stop shouting. Arnaud? He's a special needs teacher. He'll shout so much I'll want to make holes in his voice. Little holes. For little pauses. It'll always be a day like before. Labels, boxes, labels, boxes, labels . . . Always, always.

I'll go back home, Mummy wasn't there. Just my daddy. Phew, Mummy was still in the train. I don't want to die because of my ears. Her voice goes all the way to the back, it goes into my veins where they give me the injections, and it ends up in my heart. Sometimes, it'll stop beating because her voice is spiky. That's it.

I do some drawing in the bedroom if I was getting bored. Colour drawings. That way my head will be with the colours and I wasn't hearing Mummy's voice any more. Then Tani will come home, he pushes the door hard.

Tani had blood on his face, he wouldn't even notice; Daddy is laughing in front of the television. My brother came into the boys' bedroom. I'll put some alcohol on him that stings when you've got a cut and I put some plasters on him too, from the ads. Superhero plasters. My favourites. I'll put them on my fingers at HUW because the labels cut me. Tani is nice to me. He'll give me a cuddle to say thank you for the plasters. He's strange that day, his mouth smells nasty and he was crying. He'll say lots of times: 'She went behind my back!'

After Tanièl, I'll have gone out. Because if somebody hits him, I was defending him too. He always defends me. He's a nice big brother. I had followed him. He'd been at

Jojo the Terrible's. That's it. I'd have hidden myself on the other side to watch him. He'll be with the candy-pink girl. Phew. No fighting.

After, she'd have gone. I'd have put my Game Boy in my bag. I should be able to kill the final boss soon. Then Tani left the bar. I was going to wait a bit and then go back home to play as well, Jojo doesn't say anything to me. I'd even have played on the pinball machine a bit and I'd put my Game Boy on the table in front of the mirror and I had left it there.

After that I'll have made a mistake, I'd go to HUW again instead of home. Because I forgot. I wouldn't have seen it was already dark and I would be a bit scared. I'd only be thirteen. It was like I was going back to work. They call it an 'apprenticeship' but it's work.

So I went back to the Balto that would be all locked up. But my Game Boy had stayed there.

It'll be a shame. I want to beat the record, I'll nearly be at level 4 of the game where the little monkey will go jumping on the trees to get to the final boss, that's it. And I'll know that Jojo could throw my game in the bin, easy-peasy, because he'll be nasty and he didn't like me. Then I'll go all the way round the bar to find the door that'll be behind. Jojo doesn't lock that one. I knew it because if the policeman will bring me back home when it's dark, he comes this way.

I'll decide to push the door and it opens very quietly. I was poking my head round to see, there'll be some light on. I walk down the little corridor, it'll smell of rats and wee-wee. I'll go to the stockroom as well, there are big piles of newspapers and boxes and bags of dry cat food. But Jojo hadn't got a cat. It's like you'll have a pair of swimming trunks but you never get into a swimming pool. That's it.

Then, I did see Jojo, I'll just poke my head round the door so he won't see me and he wasn't getting angry at me. I'd seen him making himself look nice. He'll have used some of that sticky stuff that makes your hair go shiny and then he has a comb in his pocket and he got it out for his hair. And then, because I'll be fat, I'll make some noise and Jojo will hear me. He'll have seen me, and his eyes will be black and very small. He'll scare me. I said: 'It's my Game Boy that'll stay here, I'm taking it and I'm going, that's it.'

But it'll be weird because for the first time Jojo wasn't angry.

'Oh! It's just you, the Spaz . . . You gave me the heebie-jeebies! Sit down over there, handicap kid! Grab a chair.'

'I'm well. I'm not handicapped.'

'No harm in calling you that!! You can't say anything in this country these days. A spazzer is a spazzer. It's not nasty, don't go getting into a huff.'

'I won't get into a huff. I'll just want to take my Game Boy. That's it'

'Look, don't be annoyed. Stay a bit, come on, let's have a chat. Whaddya know, I fancy a chat this evening . . . After all the crap I have to listen to round here . . . Come on, what the hell, I've had a few drinks and I fancy a chat, that's all. Don't go thinking I'm a paedophile or something . . . Why are you scared? Come on, grab a seat! Don't you fancy a chat with Jojo?'

'All right. You will chat, you first.'

'What's your name anyway?'

'Yeznig. That's my name.'

'Well, no one's given you any breaks there, my friend. Dump a name like that on a kid, small wonder he turns out handicapped! Now, I know you're not the talkative sort but you could make an effort here. It's my last round, big boy: shall I get you a glass of grenadine?'

'Yes. All right. Grenadine's really tasty.'

'Just stay for one glass and after that you can take your game and clear off, if that's what you want. It's late, I suppose your mother'll be getting worried.'

'All right.'

'You know your brother did it again this afternoon? Gave his little Arab pal a good thrashing. What got into him?'

'He had cried. He will be sad.'

'He lands himself in the shit. He's bloody stupid.'

'No, sad.'

'Why doesn't he go to school, for starters?'

'Why will there be bottles hanging upside down behind you?'

'Er . . . dunno. Never thought about it. What are you asking me that for? Didn't anyone ever tell you not to answer a question with another question? That's just the way it is. You pour the drinks from upside down, that's all . . . Take that pastis for example, you serve it like that, with the neck facing down. Go on, drink your grenadine. I've even stuck a straw in.'

'The doctor will be cross if I was drinking grenadine. He says it would be bad, I'm a fatty. And there will be sugar in the grenadine.'

'You what? What's all this nonsense? What's your doctor's name?'

'Robin-Redbreast-Big-Test-Bluetwist-Whitemist . . . '

'Come again?'

'It'll be to remember somebody's name when it goes out of my head. Ah, here it is, it's going to come back, the name is: Doctor Blacksmith.'

'You're a funny fellow, aren't you ... ? Anyway, I reckon you're talking about Black-smith, Doctor Denis Blacksmith ... Well, let me tell you something: for someone who dispenses advice he hasn't got a leg to stand on. I wouldn't give him six months before he snuffs it from cirrhosis of the liver! Next time he makes one of his comments, you tell him: 'It's the pot calling the kettle black.' You could even say it's from me! D'you understand what it means?'

'No.'

'Too bad. Say it to that shitface anyway. If there's one thing you know how to do, it's being a parrot. Go on, repeat it!'

'It's the pot calling the kettle black.'

'Tell me ... can you keep a secret? If I told you something, you wouldn't say anything?'

'No. Nothing.'

'So it's agreed. It'll stay between you and me?'

'Yes. All right.'

He'll have told me a big secret. Shhhhh.

And then it was all over. When my tummy will have started churning, I'd run to the grass behind the pharmacy and I'd been sick.

I would have heard a noise and then nothing. Just Mummy's voice would have come from behind me and it got mixed up in the sick. Mummy will have looked for me, she picked me up. At home, I would have washed my mouth out because there was still sick and Mummy's voice on the inside. I'd count my teeth to see if I would have lost one and I was sleeping because I would be tired. Tani wouldn't be there yet.

No, I wouldn't say the secret because it's a secret. You must never tell a secret. For example, I'd have seen Arnaud at HUW, he had touched Camélia in secret in the corner, she's bigger than me, but she was deaf, poor girl, and also she doesn't talk at all. So I will have seen them and Arnaud will tell me not to tell anyone, that it would be a secret. That's it.

That's why he will buy me lot of games for my Game Boy because Mummy thinks they would be too expensive. She'll say: 'I'd have to sell the hide off my backside to buy you those things.' That's it. Arnaud gives me games to keep the secret.

No. I wasn't telling Joël's secret. No. I don't want a Nintendo DS. I just want the ski game for my Game Boy, the one where you have to do two somersaults to win the trophy.

France 3, Paris Region

More on the Making-Ends-Meet story. Since the announcement, a few days ago, that no break-in occurred on the night of the murder, and none of the day's takings were stolen, the settling of scores is looking an increasingly likely motive. According to a source close to the investigation, the findings of the forensic police and the key testimony of a mentally disabled teenager may lead to a swift outcome, as confirmed by Officer Vincent Bergues, who had this to say: 'In consideration of those elements pertaining to the investigation and without ruling out the possibility of a foul crime, a settling of scores is currently our preferred lead. But may I take this opportunity to remind you that the investigation is still under way and therefore it is impossible for me to be entirely affirmative in consideration of your question? Thank you.'

Jacques, aka Jacko, the Old Man or Hubby

So, this business of yours is still dragging on? I'm not wrong there. You've got a point. Nobody's above suspicion. We all have our dark side. Even you, I bet.

Not that I mind. Got nothing better to do. I could come here every day if you had new questions for me. I've a few new things to tell you since last time, as it happens.

First of all, and let's start with the good news, you've got the new Jacko in front of you. New man. Fresh off the shelf, I've got a meeting afterwards with a legal adviser; I'm hoping she's a looker. I want some advice off her about divorce. I got the idea from talking to my eldest. There are loads of people who get divorced after fifty, you know. I'd already thought about it, but it's hard taking risks at my age. I want to start my life over, from scratch. Want to have projects and ambitions. Going to kick off by phoning *Change Your Look*. They'll fix me up good as new from head to toe. You won't recognise me, I swear. I'll be all handsome for *Who Wants the*

Wonga?, a brand-new concept. They selected the candidates in January and guess what . . . I've been picked! I'm too excited to sleep, captain. I think about it all the time. I'm like a cat on hot bricks. Of course, I've got to start doing some exercise too. If I go on *Change Your Look*, it'd be good to drop a size or two. I've been branded a size XXL for too long. Ever since that business with the overalls hanging up in the factory locker room. One day, my label was sticking out and Marcel started laughing his head off about that XXL, just to wind me up. For a while, size XXL was written up where we clock in, instead of my name. I didn't hold it against Marcel. The factory lads just like having a good laugh, they didn't really . . . Those were the good old days.

So anyway, if I manage to get through the first round of *Who Wants the Wonga?*, I can clear off with five thousand euros. Can you imagine? With money like that, I'd beat it. A cruise up the Nile. I'll be checking out the bikinis, captain, I can tell you. I've got years to catch up on!

It was a good thing you called me in today, I'm feeling better, more ready to talk . . . Yes . . . well, I was a bit depressed, that's why I didn't say much.

Gotcha. Jacko left out a few details, you're

not wrong there . . .

About the fifteen thousand euros? I think you'd have done the same. Fifteen thousand euros is a shed-load of money. It wouldn't be right to let something like that drop. Remember what I said the other day? I ran into my kid and then we went jogging together . . . Well, I stopped there . . . I just want to make it clear that everything I said before is accurate.

So here we go. At about two thirty, give or take, we started heading home — it was late, and it was cold. I didn't want to make matters any worse, seeing as I already had the Leprosy waiting for me. I'm talking about Yéva, you'll have got that . . .

Truth is, my kid's fast out of the blocks, he was the one who got me all fired up, and my nerves were already shot to pieces. That kid's got a problem, he flies off the handle, so when I told him about the Banco ticket Joël had nicked from me, Tanièl went nuts. Really nuts. To be honest with you, it was the first time I'd seen him like that. 'We're gonna fuck his race over,' he kept saying again and again. The kid was all pumped up, he was on for doing anything to get that dough back. Basically, I got carried away by this manly surge of energy my son triggered, and I decided to follow him. I mean, come off it, it was now or never to boost my fortunes as a father and show a bit of courage for once. I know it wasn't a smart move, captain. I should've set an example and persuaded the kid not to behave like a fool ... But I couldn't help it.

We were hot-footing it over to the Balto so fast I was panting like a buffalo. 'Wait! Don't be in such a rush,' I says to the kid. We'd just done two laps of the park, I couldn't take any more.

The idea was to wake him up. Give him a bit of a scare. Nothing nasty.

We managed to get in round the back; the door was open. I was surprised a bloke like that didn't lock up properly at night. The kid and I went up the staircase leading directly to his flat. We didn't want to hurt him, it was just a case of neighbours getting their own back. I want to be clear about this: it was never our intention to kill him. To scare the pants off him, that, yes.

Not very big his place. And filthy with it. Empty bottles lying around everywhere. The kid said it smelt of dead rat. But I'll tell you what, he had a sodding great library of porn mags. Collector level, we're talking. A sodding pervert.

Then we noticed these glass jars on the sideboard, with labels on. Like we were in a

111

film or something. The scene: a murky laboratory. And the tarts on the covers of those dirty mags were looking us straight in the eye, or that's how it seemed to me . . . I asked my son to turn them over, didn't like the way they were staring at me. I knew Morvier was weird, but I hadn't realised how weird. In red writing on the labels was YÉVA. My wife's name. It was like a slap in the face. The kid couldn't get over it either. No stopping his anger now. He gets hot under the collar if a bloke so much as winks at his mum in the street, so . . .

What was inside the jars? You're never going to believe this . . . cigarette butts. The fag ends from cigarettes Yéva'd smoked. I know, because I spotted the lipstick marks on them. I'd recognise that lipstick in a thousand. She's been wearing the same one for years. So, he'd been drooling over my wife and I hadn't even realised — what a moron! She goes there every day to buy her packet of Gauloise Blondes. If I didn't know Yéva the way I do, I might've thought she was cheating on me. But nothing ever happened, bet my life on it. Morvier isn't her type.

Anyway, thing is, there was no sign of the Rink in his flat. So we went straight back downstairs again, through the stockroom to get to the bar. My idea was to find a different way of getting my own back. I wanted to pinch all the scratchcards. There had to be at least one winning ticket in that lot. Well, we walked into the bar and that's when I saw something that'll stay with me for the rest of my days. As for the position his body was in . . . Why was he starkers, anyway? When I saw his clothes piled up on the stool, I reckoned they must've raped him or something, before doing that to him. Any case, our plan had been blown out the water. Me and the kid were in complete shock. We left the way we came in, careful not to tread in the pool of blood. We had a hunch this story was going to cause us a few problems. That's why I didn't want to tell you everything last time. We didn't do anything. Even if we'd wanted to, we were too late.

Tanièl, aka Tani, Turkey Boy or Lazy Bugger

So, it seems like my old man's spilled the beans already, sir. At the end of the day, yeah, he was right. Now I've had time to think about it, I guess my idea wasn't so smart. I was the one who told him to keep quiet about that part. Didn't want no trouble. My dad's an honest guy, for real. He can be a plonker sometimes, but he's honest. I dunno what else to say.

If you look at it one way, it's a good thing we found Jojo already out cold, because I was fucking mad at him. I swear, I was ready to merk him. So at least it stopped me getting into deep shit.

But, man, was I stunned to see him like that. I mean with his mouth closed, for once. I'm kidding, sir . . . I'm just trying to play it down. I had nightmares coz of what I saw. A dead guy, stark naked, stabbed all over, practically floating in his own blood. It's not every day you see that kind of thing. It's shocking, innit? Even for me — and I ain't the sensitive type — it made a big impression.

You've got to remember the guy was a caveman, his head was mashed. I mean, what kind of person collects a woman's cigarette butts and displays them in glass jars? Hey? I'm arksing you . . . He'd actually labelled those things and gone and categorised them by month, November to February. When I saw my old lady's name written up like that, I flipped. So once we were downstairs, with all that smell of blood, forget it! Fucking pool of fucking blood! Don't even go there. We didn't say nothing. Just stared into space. I'm telling you, we got out of there, and fast. It must've been between half past two and three in the morning. We were scared of the Feds turning up and even more scared of bumping into the guy who did it. Me and the old man were a wimp-out.

On the way home, I told my old man we'd have to keep it between the two of us. Gotta say, I mean, I don't know if he told you or anything, but he was panicking big time. More like his usual self. I shouldn't have led him on. He needed to prove something to me. Making out he was ready to take on Jojo, you get me? I sussed he was just doing it for me. But I already know my old man's a brave guy. No need to put on a show. Anyhow, there's something my dad didn't notice to begin with, and that was the shotgun on the bookshelf. I spotted Jacko zooming in on the porn mags right next to it. It was one of those old-fashioned guns, we're talking massive. Magalie's old man's got the same in his attic. So I held the Rink's weapon for a bit, I was pretending to aim and everything. Makes you look class, I reckon. But Jacko gave me a hard time about it. 'Don't touch it! You're crazy!' So I put it back. I'm telling you that for the fingerprints . . . I know you'll have gone over the Rink's flat from top to bottom, you and your team. You must've collected my fingerprints, no?

Yeah, thought so. You're on target then, just as well I told the truth. I could've been accused, innit. And you know what, sir . . . I could've done it. I wanted to tell you that. You don't know how far you'll go 'til you've been there. I could've, but I didn't — that's what matters.

I'm telling you this as well because I'm thinking about what Magalie would've done. She'd have gone over to the bad side . . . What was she planning to come up with next time? Someone dying? War? Rape?

I never thought she'd do nothing like that. Making up a baby. She deserves one big fat slap, man. Like a jerk, I believed her story. Didn't know what to do with myself, I was all over the place. So there you go, I've finished with her because of that pregnancy test business, simple as. She can cry all she likes, just means she'll piss less, as my old lady would say. If I was her, I'd have come up with another excuse, wriggled out of it somehow, but I'd never fess up. I'd say I lost the baby or, I dunno, that I was in the 0.1 per cent. You get me? Something, anything . . . It's too weird putting yourself in a wifey's shoes, and it's worse when the wifey's as loopy as her.

It's risky, man, letting the air out of a lie as big as that one. I don't know what's inside her head, but I don't reckon there's much apart from maybe a chickpea. She's ruined everything.

Not that I care, she pissed me off and we weren't into the same shit. And anyway, when it comes to blondes, I can have as many as I like, they're too easy.

She's the kind of girl who's used to dumping guys: she'd never been ditched before me. It was her first time. She's so predictable. Telling everybody she's the one who chucked me. I was so sure that's what she'd do, I recorded the whole thing on my mobile. I'm no liar. Listen . . . Does this have anything to do with the investigation? You bet.

'You'll be sorry, you'll see. The day you come back to me, you'll feel like a total loser. You'll beg me on your knees to take you back. But I'm not the kind of girl you can recycle . . . Once you've chucked me, you'll never get me back!'

'Yeah, whatever. Scratch my balls, like I give a toss. Don't wanna stay with a big fat liar, you get me?'

'Ha-llo! What about when you drink? You're the liar round here! Look, I came here to tell you the truth because I was, like, feeling bad about it — and this is how you thank me? You guys make me laugh, you're all the same. I was going to chuck you sooner or later, anyway. You're not in my league. The day you see me on TV, when I'm in Hollywood, you'll be crying into your mum's miniskirt!'

'Go on then, clear off . . . '

'Yeah, yeah, I'm leaving, OK? But first you've got to give me my money back. You'd better cough up and, like, superquick or I'll tell my dad, I'm warning you — '

'Oh, so now you've suddenly remembered your darling daddy? I'll give you your bills back, so don't start with the long face. And next time you decide to be pregnant, get your act together . . . I hope at least you'll know who the dad is.'

She needed a reality check, you get me? If she goes on flaunting it like that, everyone'll just turn their backs on her. That's life, innit?

You know what, sir, at least something good's coming out of this whole business. I'm taking myself in hand, trying to think of me now. Because, fuck me, I'm telling you, I was bricking it big time, picturing Tani as a stay-at-home dad already, like my old man. With Magalie getting back from work every evening to shout at me and all that shit . . . Me looking after the brat. Nightmare. Just like my parents.

It's cool with my old man, he wants to go with me to see the educational advisers. I wasn't feeling it to go on my own, plus I'll fess up to being kind of scared, innit. They're going to help me find a college or training or whatever. I've got to get a move on: what my old man said the other evening has really stuck in my head. I'll support him, even if he wants to leave my old lady. He's missed out on a lot of stuff and I know I don't want to do the same. We're not condemned to failure, or life would be one big fucking injustice.

Magalie Fournier, aka the Blonde, the Slut or Turkey Boy's Wifey

I'm not very good company today, officer. I'm feeling *blue*. I know you can't see I'm sad because I'm wearing my everyday concealer. To add to my stress, my period started yesterday and I'm not using the same tampons as usual. OMG, I'm like totally out of sync. But don't worry about it, stop pulling that face, it's no big deal, I'm hanging on in there, LOL.

So, basically, what happened is, I've dumped Tani. We're not together any more. What d'you mean, this isn't getting off to a good start? OK, all right, seeing as it's you I don't care, *whatever*, the truth is, he's the one who ditched me. How crazy is that? Like, totally mental. See, you're blown away too! I can see from your face you're gobsmacked. I know exactly what you're thinking: 'How can you ditch a girl like that?' I won't pretend I don't share your concern . . .

Anyway, I'm here to finish giving you my account, aren't I?

I'm a chatty kind of girl, as you'll have noticed, and there's only one thing I've kept to myself, which is that before college, like so early in the morning, before it was even properly light, I'd come by to piss in front of the Balto's shutters. A long, piping hot piss that I made splash on purpose. I did it for a week. My way of getting my own back. It blew my mind, just knowing that fat perverted wanker was going to walk on my piss and spread it everywhere, LMHO.

You don't think it's funny? No . . . hmm . . . OK, I see.

Well, get this, officer, I didn't find always being called a whore very funny, either, especially in front of my guy. It wound me up big time, I can tell you. I *am* sixteen, you know. Plus, he reported everything back to my dad. You'd think he was working for him. I swear to you, it wouldn't surprise me. My old man's got no idea what to do with his money, so it's totally possible he paid Joël to spy on me. Because of all his grassing me up, they confiscated my phone and shut me in my bedroom. Life at home was no picnic before, but after that it was, like, unbearable. I had to run away if I wanted to go out. When my mum tells me her stories about May '68, Liberty & Co., I tell her to get lost. To me, '68 is, like, prehistory, plus, if they're so into freedom, what are they doing shutting me in my bedroom?

Joël deserved what happened to him, I really believe that. Why don't you just put the handcuffs on me? Go on, arrest me, I'm a minor, I'll get out soon enough! I'm telling you, prison would be a lot better than home at the moment. It's such a nightmare.

D'you remember how I told you I went home the other evening after seeing Tanièl? Well, the truth is I cancelled my Tektonik party for the simple reason that my idiot folks were still there. Slumped in the living room like a pair of noodles. When I saw their funeral faces, I thought I was gonna *die*. I wanted to scream out. Smash everything. Rip it all to shreds. In the end, my mum explained she'd called her shrink and he'd told her it wasn't such a good idea to leave me on my own for three days after all. We're talking the same shrink who'd said what a brilliant initiative it was last week, because it'd, like, give me this big sense of responsibility. My bitch of a *mom*, with that facelift of hers — if you ask me she's got a dead-fish expression now. She sees me more like a study case than her own child these days, and all because of her shrinks and those shitty books she's got. I wanted to *die*. The only thing left to do was head over to Brico

Depot and buy eight metres of rope to hang myself with, out of sight, in the attic.

So I ran up to my room, switched on my computer — the password's always the same: *sexy bomb*. I alerted everyone via MSN the party was *no-go*. It was, like, top priority before someone showed up and found out the real deal. Otherwise, the next day at college, it'd be like total guaranteed *shame*.

I watched some stupid stuff on TV and ate a tub of ice cream. That's what all the American stars do when they're sad. Then, I switched on my mobile, because I knew I'd have, like, so many disappointed messages . . . but whaddya know, nothing. Not a single missed call, not even a text. That's how I found out, by MSN again, that fat slag Karine Z had organised an *alternative* party round at hers. To get her own back on me, because she was so mad about not being invited to mine. She'd even got a load of alcohol in as bait. I couldn't believe my eyes when I read what she'd posted on MySpace: 'Don't have a crap night at Magalie's! Chill at mine instead. Who needs her 'get-together'? Just head for my *fiesta*!' What a bitch. Plus, she even tried to make it rhyme, like *who* does she think she is? A poet or something? 'Get-together . . . get-together . . . ' what's that supposed to mean? That I throw kids' tea parties? My nerves were, like, all over the place. Should've been smarter than her. Yes, officer, I'm getting there, but it's important you understand what kind of state I was in. I cried a lot, of course. I'm beautiful when I cry, you know, or at least that's what loads of guys have told me. If I sit in a cafe, somewhere that's not the Balto of course, and I start crying, I can guarantee you, one hundred per cent, someone'll chat me up. I mean, it's not like I've got to cry for that to happen, but if I do cry then it's like a bonus. I come across as soft and vulnerable, the kind of girl who needs a male shoulder to lean on. Guess where I got that from? From *HC* — *Hot & Cute* — of course.

You're going to end up finding out about all my tricks. You should subscribe to *HC*. LOL.

It must've been about one o'clock in the morning when I decided on the escape of the century. This time, I was ready, I wouldn't chicken out. I got a few things ready to take with me, just the really vital stuff: a change of underwear and my *make-up bag*. Can you believe it filled a whole suitcase? It was mega-heavy. Have you ever tried running away with a suitcase that weighs fourteen kilos? Well, there you go. It was harsh. I didn't take it with me in the end. I walked down

Acacia Street, and then across the housing estate. It weirded me out — it was deserted and I was thinking of all those rape stories you hear about. What if it happened to me? Not that it'd come as a big surprise, or anything. I'm a rapist's dream victim. Put yourself in his place, OK? So he comes across a girl like me ... Well, he'd never rape anybody else after that, would he, because it'd be, like, impossible to do any better. Forget it, officer, it's just this crazy thought I had. So I headed for the Balto because I needed a bit of comfort, I was *down*. After the botched party, I needed Tanièl's arms to bury my face in.

But anyway, seeing as we're talking about it again and we're playing the honesty game, I'm going to explain everything, even if I do sound like a snitch. Plus, it's not like I've got to cover for his family any more, now he's dumped me. I don't have to be faithful or loyal, I don't owe him anything, in fact I don't give a shit. As I got to the front of the Balto, I saw two people leaving by the back door. Of course I recognised them. Like I've already said, everybody knows everybody round here. Plus those two are hardly difficult to recognise. LOL.

It was Tanièl's mum leading her son by the hand. I mean, her other son, the autistic one.

They were practically running, so that got me interested. I hid, and as soon as they were a bit further off, I went in through the same door — I'd never noticed it before. And then, well, you know what I saw next. Oh my God, it was hideous. It was the first time I'd seen an old man naked. I was, like, totally shocked. It shouldn't be allowed. It was DIS-GUS-TING, and I *so* mean that.

It was lucky I hadn't brought my fourteen-kilo suitcase, or it'd have got in the way of me running my ass off. I'm not drawing any conclusions, I'm just telling you what I saw. By the way, has Tani already come by here? What d'you mean you're not allowed to answer my question?

It won't change anything, you know. It's so over between us.

Yéva, aka Madame Yéva, My Marge or My Old Lady

Listen, commander sweetheart, from where I'm sitting I've already told you everything. And it's not just from where I'm sitting — I really *have* told you everything. You're sweet, so all I can imagine is you've called me back in because you've been thinking about me a lot, you took a shine to me the other day and you want to take me out for dinner. Tell me I'm wrong!

Oh well, at least I tried.

Because, and let me say this one more time, I have other fish to fry. I've got a job to hold on to. Except it's not really a job any more, since the temp took over the disputed cases. That dickhead Joseph Frédéric's just taking the piss. Doesn't give me anything to do these days. He's trying to make me crack, but he won't succeed, that I can guarantee. I can absorb more than a Spontex. I've rumbled my female boss, and as for the men, I know them like the back of my hand. I can spot their little schemes even with my eyes shut, I could write an encyclopedia about them.

127

I keep on turning up to work with a smile. Especially in front of Patricia and Simone. I want to show them it'll take a lot more to get me down. Oh, and I'm putting my days to good use: filing the archive material. It's one hell of a mess, going back to 1997. There's a lot I'm finding out as I file those invoices. I'll tell you what, our previous boss sprayed the booze about before leaving, and that's for sure. I mean, can you believe it? What world are we living in? As my poor father — may he rest in peace — used to say: 'Injustice gets all the luck'! I had to thump the table for a crappy thirty-six-euro pay rise last year. So maybe that explains why I feel a sharp pain in the backside every time I find four-star hotel bills and restaurant tabs for 325 euros? I'm making photocopies and putting them to one side, for the time being. I'm preparing my defence. On the quiet.

If I've understood properly, I'm here to clarify some of the things I said last time. Are you doing this for all the people you've interviewed? OK. Just some, including me. What else do you want to know? I don't like repeating things a hundred thousand times. I have to do enough of that with my kids and my husband. So please, commander sweetheart, spare me.

Now *that*, for instance, is something I've

already explained to you. Let's start again. I found Yeznig, my kid, being sick against the wall behind the pharmacy. More details — like what? The colour of his puke? What he'd eaten beforehand? If there were any bits in it? Time-wise, I'd say it was one thirty in the morning, or thereabouts. I've got no idea what made him sick, he simply told me he had tummy ache. So when we got back home, I gave him something to settle it. The pharmacy, commander sweetheart, is opposite the Balto, as I'm sure you know: you've visited the site.

Yes, that's right, I noticed the bar was closed already. The shutters were down and there wasn't a soul around. Oh yes, there's something I forgot to tell you, which is that the lights were on inside. I did notice that.

Commander sweetheart, humour me here . . . We are in the land of truth and justice here, aren't we? France? With a capital F, the way I pictured it when I was a girl?

Sorry? What d'you mean you're not sure? Thanks a lot. Nice of you to rub it in. Then again, I should've expected an answer like that. You're still a policeman, after all . . . and, don't get me wrong, but being hopeful isn't exactly part of your job description.

One thing's for certain, we may be in the land of human rights but it's sure as hell not the land of poor people's rights. If I had any money, I'd be somewhere else, far away from this town of losers, and I wouldn't be mixed up in any of this.

Look, if you want the real story then, all right, I'll tell you everything. I was scared. OK. I got the fright of my life. A mother's instinct is incredibly — strong. It squeezes your insides, it knots your stomach and tugs at your guts. You don't use your brain at times like that. It's the same for all mothers, even female gorillas. D'you ever watch those late-night wildlife documentaries? I love them. When the old boy drops the remote and starts snoring I put them on. They fascinate me. Female gorillas and she-wolves will kill to protect their babies. I find that very moving, commander sweetheart. It's nature getting its way. Our instincts kick in.

To be honest, to start with, I was convinced that son of a bitch Morvier had given him something to drink. My Yeznig can't take alcohol, he only drinks fruit juice and grenadine. And anyway, he's still a kid. When I saw him in that state, I thought he was sloshed. He was opposite the bar. What kind of nutter would be stupid or evil enough to make a thirteen-and-a-half-year-old disabled child drink alcohol? Morvier. It's what you might call a logical conclusion, commander sweetheart. He was the only person I could think of. With that leery face of his. His dirty remarks and his pervert's eyes. Grabbing my baby by the hand, I clacked my heels over to those shutters. I banged as hard as I could. I banged and banged again, calling out: 'Open up! Open up, you son of a bitch! I'm going to skin you alive, you bastard! Open up, I want to slit your throat!'

Now, I'm going to make a confession here: if he'd opened his bloody metal shutters, I would've done it, and I'm not kidding. Morvier had it coming to him from everyone, and I'd have done the deed. But he didn't open up, did he? I asked my son if he felt better. He said yes and would I tidy my voice away in my pocket. You see, my baby has this funny way of explaining things. I know he doesn't really like me shouting, it puts him in a bad mood. So I apologised. 'Sorry, sorry, my baby, I won't shout any more, promise!' That's when he showed me the stockroom door. We tiptoed inside and went down a corridor that led to the bar. It was full of smoke so I . . . I didn't see everything . . . straight away. It was already starting to stink, it was terrible. I didn't tell you all of this before because I was frightened for my baby. He's a minor, he's retarded, you can see where I'm coming from. He's not capable of something like that. And anyway, my baby isn't violent, I guarantee you. When he was little, he used to bring us injured pigeons to look after. He even kept a shoebox in the garden with all his first-aid kit inside. He liked making cuts and bruises better. He's an unusual child, I'll grant you that, commander sweetheart, but you've seen him, he's gentle. He wouldn't hurt a fly. I know he's a bit big for his age, but he gets that from my side of the family. In Armenia, our men have big moustaches and they're built like oxen. They're men. Real ones.

He couldn't do anything to Jojo. Are you following me? It can't be him. I'm his mother, I know him better than anybody.

You found a DNA sample? Where? On the knife handle . . . And you're telling me now! So what? As far as I know, that doesn't prove anything. There's no CCTV in that bloody bar! Until I've seen the pictures to prove it, I refuse to believe any of this. You're making a mistake! This is a miscarriage of justice!

How dare you say that kind of bullshit to my face? Of course I know justice doesn't need a CCTV camera to be upheld . . . But maybe it doesn't work so well, after all. There must be some misunderstanding. Perhaps he did hold the knife . . . and . . . so what? You're trying to destabilise us but you won't succeed. I heard a noise when we were inside the bar, and I didn't make that up. There was a gang on the prowl. We heard voices and engines too. Motorbikes, I think. I didn't see them but I heard them. I bet it was them. I know it wasn't my son. What are you making him out to be? A murderer?

Anyway, as I've said before, Morvier's no loss. Far from it. And even if my baby did kill him, he'd deserve a medal! We'd have rid our country of one fat bastard. And let me tell you, there's plenty more on my fat bastard list who deserve to kick the bucket too. My son should be awarded the *Légion d'honneur*!

Nadia and Ali Chacal, aka the Twins, the Marseille Posse or the Jackals

— Officer, our parents are having a really hard time with all this. They're scared stiff. We don't want any trouble, please. We're minors and they're the ones who pay for our mistakes 'til we're eighteen. I swear I didn't know anything. As usual, it's the crackpot here who's causing us problems. I've got no idea how we spent nine months together in the same womb without pulling each other's eyes out.

— All right, that's enough. Let me explain. Basically, yeah, when you called us in again, it didn't surprise me. I guessed you would, and I decided to explain everything to my family. We always stand by each other. They needed to know before you did. She's right. She didn't know anything. I kept it all to myself.

— Stand by each other, yeah, right! Dragging us into all your dodgy business.

— We got overheard, I'm sure of that. There was someone behind the metal shutters, they were making a noise. But that doesn't mean I've got anything to do with this, you know. It's a dirty affair. Anyway, getting back to the fight. I'm a proud person. As we say where we come from, I've got *nif*, you know, pride, a 'nose'.

— No kidding, you've got a nose all right . . . What? Don't look at me like that . . .

— I got my face smashed in, good and proper. I couldn't just let it drop. He takes my girl, he makes mincemeat of me, and — what, nothing? I had to get back at him. Basically, yeah, what I didn't say is that I woke up about one o'clock in the morning. Everyone was asleep in the house. I had a hangover, and my head was killing me. It weighed a tonne, my head. So did the anger pumping through me. I got dressed quietly and left by the back door. In Marseille, our old flat was on the ninth floor, so I wouldn't have been able to split in the middle of the night like that. I went down Parmentier Walk, on the estate, to see my crew. There were three of them, sitting outside — life's not easy for them, you know, they're there whatever the weather. Three friends. No, I'm not giving you their names. I'm just telling you what happened, that's all.

— Oh my days! So now you're playing at best *gadjo*? You're so full of shit!

— I didn't even need to tell them what'd

happened, they were already linked in. That kinda news travels fast.

I warmed them up a bit and then they were ready to follow me. I even bigged up the story. I made it so Turkey Boy was like the most *wanted* person on the estate. We were out to get our revenge. We made it as far as the pharmacy on their mopeds. I was riding behind one of the *gadjos* and he'd smoked so much spliff he lost his grip on the handlebars. We skidded on something weird. Vomit, I think. The moped overturned and we went with it. That's where these grazes on my elbow come from. I didn't get them from the fight. I lied to the doctor.

— What about the grazes to your brain, how'd you get them?

— Shut it. So that's it, officer. The Balto was closed. Which surprised me. I was sure he'd be there with the blonde. But there was nothing going down. No blonde, no bar, nothing. I went over and that's when I heard footsteps behind the shutters.

We believe in *jnouns*. There's this invisible world humans can't see. Like a parallel life. My mum's got loads of stories on that front. There might even be some in this room, right next to you. Some of them mean well and others are out to harm you. It depends.

OK, so it's like *big shame* to admit it, but

the noise behind the shutters made all of us jump. My mates, where they come from, they've got the same stories about *jnouns*. We picked up the mopeds again, fast as greased lightning. Seeing as they were all stoned, I guess they were flipping out even more than I was. We didn't hang around to find out more. I just made a mental note to settle the score with Turkey Boy later. When we'd started out, the three *gadjos* from Parmentier were up for getting him out of bed. They even asked if they could bang his girl. But after those weird noises, we got the jitters. And we turned back again. So, you see, I wasn't even thinking about Joël right then. Far as I was concerned, he was just another racist. Turkey Boy's head was what I wanted.

— He's the one who killed the racist. It was the Turk. I know it. He's got a murderer's face.

— Stop talking bullshit. Nobody asked you. My blud would never kill anyone. It's not his style. He's a good *gadjo*, in spite of everything. He'd never do anything like that.

— No . . . Go figure . . . One moment he wants to smash his face in, and the next he's standing up for him!

— I hope this won't cause us any problems, officer. I've got dreams, ambitions for my career. I want to be an actor. As soon as I've got enough dough, I'll get my nose fixed and try out for the big screen. I don't want to screw everything up with a criminal record.

—Yeah, well, if you ask me, when you mess up, you take responsibility and you pay for it. At least if he goes to prison, I'll get his bedroom for a while, it's bigger.

— You think you're so smart, don't you? Honest, officer, now you know everything. Good luck with the rest of the investigation ... But I'm telling you, we've got nothing to do with it. It's my fault. Seeing as I've got nothing to hide, I should've told you everything the first time round. Can you talk to my mum, please? She was crying just now. I hate seeing her like this.

Yeznig, aka Baby, Fatty or the Spaz

I'll have seen my mummy who's crying. She'll be sad. My cheek's a bit dirty and I hate it when she'd wipe me with her saliva. Do all mummies do it? Take a tissue, wet it with their tongue and wipe your cheek? It's dirty if you asked me. She'll have told me that mummy birds used to chew the food in their mouths and after they'd give it to the baby birds. That's disgusting.

Oh yes! I need to say thank you for the Game Boy game you gave me, the ski one.

Now I had to tell Joël's secret. I could say it but not to the psychiatrists. They had to leave here first. I'm only speaking to you. I didn't like the psychiatrists, just the policemen because they'd be nice to me when they'd have taken me back home at night.

They'd have left. That's it. Will I stand up to tell the story?

'Come on! Look, I'll fix you another grenadine. But when you get a taste for the old vino you won't be able to do without it, you'll see!'

'Thank you, Jojo.'

'So, mongol, tell me, if your dad asked you

139

to bump him off, would you do it?'

'I didn't know. If he'd ask nicely, yes, all right.'

'Come on then, we're going to play a fun game, you're going to hit me. Are you on?'

'No. I didn't like hitting someone. It would hurt.'

'Tell you what, my fat friend, you'd be doing me a favour. Go on, hit me! Your brother wouldn't have thought twice about it. Hard as nails, he is. You're a wet rag. Go back home. You don't know how to have fun.'

'Yes I do. I won't be a wet rag. That's not true.'

'Go on then, hit me. Look, let's strike a friendly deal. If you punch me in the face, I'll let you play on the pinball machine. My pinball for your punch.'

'Yes. All right.'

★ ★ ★

Since I won't be a wet rag, I'll have hit so I can play pinball. His face is bruised. He's bleeding but I'm stronger than my brother.

★ ★ ★

'Here, take this. Let's make up a new game. Take the knife. Hold onto it. We're going to have fun, you'll see. You're going to stab my belly all over, until I fall asleep. Are you up for that?'

'No. No. Not that. That won't be funny. I won't want to kill you.'

'See, I said you were a wet rag. If I'd asked your brother, he wouldn't have given it a second thought.'

'I know.'

'Go on, I'm telling you it's just a game! I won't be dead, I'm just going to fall asleep! Right, I'm getting undressed, look, I'm starkers! I always sleep starkers!'

And then, when it'll all be over, the knife fell to the floor. He was sleeping forever. There will be blood. Everywhere. It was disgusting. And then I run outside. My tummy's churning. I am sick.

The Parisian, Oise edition

The debate continues to rage in Making-Ends-Meet. While the town hums with rumours about the potential interrogation of the principal witness, the mother of this mentally handicapped thirteen-year-old has already complained of a 'bloody miscarriage of justice'.

In his most recent press briefing, the public prosecutor refused to talk about a 'suspect', merely confirming that what happened at the Balto, on the evening when Joël Morvier met his death, remains 'shrouded in mystery'.

Joël, aka Jojo, aka The Rink

'Shrouded in mystery'. Course it's shrouded in mystery.

There are heaps of dark memories in all our lives. Oil stains. Tangles in our heads.

Some people lie down on the shrink's couch to get rid of them, others prefer to carry the baggage. To get drunk from time to time, plug the gaps and talk about nothing. That's how it is for me. I've got plenty to complain about, I just never let on.

Uncle Louis was the only person I told, but he snuffed it before I could get him to believe me. He said my brain was all shook up and I was spouting rubbish. He took me for an ass.

You shouldn't rush to write someone off as an idiot. I know what they were thinking, all of them, every time they saw me: 'Morvier, what a rat . . . ' Truth is, nobody ever taught me to be anything else. With time and some talent, I even made a good rat. A professional rat. The potential was already there, in the froth of my gene pool.

It wasn't a hunting accident that killed my dad. I'll guarantee you that. I was there. Nobody ever wanted to believe my story. But every time I close my eyes, I can see it all over again. It wasn't long after Mum walked out on us. I'd had it up to here with what my old man used to say about her. That she was a whore who'd slept with everyone in Making-Ends-Meet, including women and animals. He didn't hold back. So, of course, I started believing I really was a son of a bitch. Which is what he'd call me, from time to time. You could say it was affectionate. That's what the old folks were like, back in the day.

I'm not such a nasty piece of work. If they'd known my dad, they'd realise I'm not in his league. Next to him, I'm gentle as a lamb, a right pansy.

One Sunday morning, while some people were getting up early to pray to their Christ, me and my dad were already combing the woods for hares. He'd promised to teach me how to shoot.

I was over the moon . . . It didn't take much to make me happy. I was just a teenager, stupid and dull, with a load of rubbish sprouting inside my skull.

We were walking through the woods; it was spitting and the damp grass smelt good. It's a smell I've always liked. I remember I kept going on at him: 'But Dad, there's no hares! I can't see a single hare round here!' And he'd say: 'Shut your face, Jojo, and keep going.'

The further we got into the woods, the more I went on at him: 'But Dad, I still can't see any hares round here.' And he'd say: 'Shut it, Jojo!'

We carried on for a while. It was wet, and that made me want to piss. So I told the old man I needed to take a leak and he asked if it could wait. I said yes, I didn't want to annoy him.

We tramped on through the sludge for at least another kilometre and then, all of a sudden, the old man said: 'Stop, we're here.'

He looked straight at me. He cleared his throat and coughed up a gob that must've weighed at least a hundred kilos. Enormous. Great big lump of spit that probably flattened a ladybird to death. The old man had gone into slow motion, and I was starting to feel scared. He took off his checked cap — it was grey, I remember that. He threw it on the ground. At first, I thought I must've cocked up again, what with him looking so annoyed. He held out his gun, which stunned me because, before that, he'd never let me touch it. It was his and his alone. The gun had replaced my mum, or as good as. I caught it and I was shocked by how heavy it was, but it was a big deal to hold it for the first time. 'So, where are the hares, Dad?' And then I asked him again, because he was behaving strange. 'Hey, Dad? Where are those hares?'

'Shut it, why don't you! Can't you forget about those bloody hares for a minute? You're going to sing with me!'

He started chanting The Marseillaise.

'Arise children of the fatherlaaann-duh . . . '

He took one step backwards.

'The day of gloooory has arriiiiive-duh . . . '

Then two, three, four, five steps.

'Against us tyraneeeey-uh's bloody banner is raaaaise-duh! Sing with me, bloody hell!'

He seemed set on the idea, so I started mumbling too.

'Tyraneeeey-uh's bloody banner is raaaaise-duh!'

He walked backwards another ten paces, but he was only five metres off, max. My old man had very short legs. No matter how much he kept retreating, he wasn't really going anywhere.

He stopped singing. 'Listen, you'll say it was an accident! D'you hear me? An accident! Go on, shoot! SHOOT ME, I'M TELLING YOU!'

He wouldn't take no for an answer. I won't go into the details but it was a while before I did it. And then, BANG! I was so petrified I pissed myself. I only fired the once. My first time. I kept the gun. It's upstairs. Never used it since. I get it out from time to time to scare

146

the kids, that's all.

Of course, everybody believed it was an accident. For two or three years, I learned all about how to run the bar with Uncle Louis, the only family I had left. Then he went and died of cancer and I was on my own. They dumped both of them in the communal grave. They never wanted a gravestone. And it'll be the same for me: communal grave. We don't care about that bollocks in our family. No grave and no stupid burial service.

I'm not telling you all this for the sympathy trip, I just wanted to get it off my chest. Plus, it needed explaining. In detail.

My idea wasn't to do any wrong by the Spaz, still less by Yéva. He just turned up at the wrong time. That evening, I'd decided it was my last round. I'd put some Brylcreem in my hair and I was nursing a bottle of Scotch. Like Elvis. It really wasn't the evening to go and forget his Game Boy, but seeing as he was there, he might as well lend a hand.

From the first punch he made me piss blood: my nose was ripped to pieces. One hell of a clout. Then he went and played four rounds of pinball. Don't know if I could've held out for the fifth. So I got the big knife from the bar drawer. But once we were got down to the serious business the kid wasn't so deft: too sensitive. He stuck it in once, clumsily, and when the blood started flowing he went all pale. Took off without looking back. Talk about a helping hand . . . I had to finish the job off myself. So I jabbed my body all over 'til I knew I was on the way out. I stuck it in at the base of my belly, in the gut, straight through my liver and everything in my past along with all the other rotten stuff inside me. Then I ditched the knife and fell to the floor, like a dead hare. I was lying in a pool of my own blood, starkers, you wouldn't believe the position I was in. Ready for curtain up.

Glossary

Banco — a brand of scratchcard

Brico-Dépot — DIY store

Charles Aznavour (born 1924) — French-Armenian singer, who got an early career break when Edith Piaf took him under her wing. In 1998 he was named Entertainer of the Century by CNN and *Time Online*, beating Elvis Presley and Bob Dylan to the title

Chorba — Middle Eastern and Maghrebi spicy soup with tomatoes and chickpeas (or sometimes vermicelli); popular during Ramadan

Conforama — household superstore

Dalida (1933–1987) — famous Egyptian-born singer of Italian origin, who spent most of her life in France

Darty — chain of electrical goods stores

Delarue's peak-time TV show (*Ça se discute*) — TV confessional programme with Jean-Luc Delarue

Dragon Ball — Japanese *manga* series by Akira Toriyama, originally published weekly (1984–1995), and later made into an animé series

Everybody's Talking About It (*On en parle*) — mid-morning TV talk show

Farandole — a lively dance from Provence (in 6/8 or 4/4 time), with dancers linking hands to form a weaving line that follows the leader

France 3 — second largest French public television channel, made up of a network of regional television services (in this instance, Paris region)

Gadjo — 'outsider' in Romany, referring to a male non-Roma, as in Tony Gatlif's film *Gadjo Dilo* (crazy outsider)

HUW (Helping Us Work) — CAT (*Centre D'Aide par le Travail*) is a real organisation, providing work placement for disabled people; HUW is an invented name but a real British equivalent would be something like WORK-STEP

Jnouns (djiins) — spirits in Arabian stories and Muslim mythology, they are less than angels, but able to appear in human or animal form and to exercise supernatural influence. The French version of *The Thousand and One Nights* translated these creatures as '*génies*', hence the English adoption of the genie

Julie Lescaut — French police television series

Making-Ends-Meet — the fictional place name in French is *Joigny-les-deux-bouts*, which means 'Joigny-in-the-sticks'; it is also a pun on the expression '*joindre les deux bouts*' or 'trying to make ends meet'

Minitel — ultimately doomed French Tele-com precursor to the Internet, this comprised a brown mini-computer connected to the tele-phone and used for bookings and general information

Oise — department 35km north of Paris, in the Picardie region, named after the river Oise. The fictional Making-Ends-Meet is not far from Oise

The Parisan (*Le Parisien*) — daily paper with a national edition called *Aujourd'hui en France*, which is the best-selling French paper

Perno — Magalie's father's Labrador is named after Jean-Pierre Pernaut, the anchorman of 13 Heures on TF1, France's flagship daytime news programme

Rapido — instant cards that cost 1 Euro

RER (*réseau express regional*) — fast regional train network connecting the *banlieue* (sub-urbs) and beyond with the city centre

Roumi — Arabic term for a white person

Skyrock FM — youth music radio station, with an emphasis on rap

Tecktonik (TCK) — frenetic street dance performed to electro music (based on a blend of techno, rave and hip-hop styles) with an emphasis on arm rather than leg movements. TCK started in the 2000s in the southern suburbs of Paris and often relies on house music imported from Northern Europe

Voici — French weekly celebrity women's magazine

We're-Not-Prostitutes-and-We-Won't-Take-It-Lying-Down *(Ni Putes Ni Soumises)* — often translated as *Neither Prostitutes nor Downtrodden*, this organisation actively defends the rights of North African women in France, in response to a culture of gang rape among some disenfranchised male youths

Translator's Thanks

This translation of *Bar Balto* was informed by a full-length scratch reading at Live Magazine, Brixton, on 11th August 2010. The parts were read by young slangstas and other willing folks, in the company of my wonderfully supportive editor Poppy Hampson. The translator would like to thank them all for their generosity and insights.

Joël: Tim Kane
Tanièl: Jason Richards
Magalie: Fiona Obadiaru
Yéva: Fiona Obadiaru
Jacques — Tim Kane
Nadia — Maeva Chandler
Ali — Mo Barrie
Yeznig — Reece Akins
Media reports: Carole Mendy

Further slang thanks to Rohan Ayinde-Smith. And to Cleo Soazandry, for always being there.

Big *remerciements* to Bill Swainson, for Making-Ends-Meet.

The excerpted translation of *The Marseillaise* is by Iain Patterson and taken from his website: http://www.marseillaise.org/english/english.html